When they pulled into the garage at Stoneview, there wasn't any light on in the cottage.

"Wait. I'll walk you to the house," Brian told Robyn.

"No need. I know the way. I'd rather say goodbye here." She surprised him by giving him a lingering kiss on the lips. Then she turned away quickly and disappeared into the shadows of the overhanging trees planted along the walk.

Brian headed in the opposite direction toward the cottage. He was only halfway there when Robyn's scream cut through the air like a knife.

Calling her name, he streaked toward the back of the house. When the porch light came into view, he saw her. She was standing at the bottom of the back stairs, shivering and staring at the screen door.

A huge funeral wreath hung there.

The flowers and leaves were dead.

Death at Stoneview was printed on a tattered black banner.

D0449744

STONEVIEW ESTATE
LEONA KARR

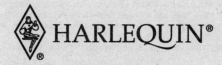

HARLEQUIN®

TORONTO • NEW YORK • LONDON
AMSTERDAM • PARIS • SYDNEY • HAMBURG
STOCKHOLM • ATHENS • TOKYO • MILAN • MADRID
PRAGUE • WARSAW • BUDAPEST • AUCKLAND

With thanks to Joan Biederman, a gracious
and generous lady who inspired this novel.
With affection to Scott McClane,
a very special and talented friend.

ISBN 0-373-22900-3

STONEVIEW ESTATE

Copyright © 2006 by Leona Karr

www.eHarlequin.com

Printed in U.S.A.

ABOUT THE AUTHOR

A native of Colorado, Leona (Lee) Karr is the author of nearly forty books. Her favorite genres are romantic suspense and inspirational romance. After graduating from the University of Colorado with a B.A. and the University of Northern Colorado with an M.A. degree, she taught as a reading specialist until her first book was published in 1980. She has been on the Waldenbooks bestseller list and nominated by *Romantic Times* for Best Romantic Saga and Best Gothic Author. She has been honored as the Rocky Mountain Fiction Writer of the Year, and received Colorado's Romance Writer of the Year Award. Her books have been reprinted in more than a dozen foreign countries. She is a presenter at numerous writing conferences and has taught college courses in creative writing.

Books by Leona Karr

HARLEQUIN INTRIGUE
120—TREASURE HUNT
144—FALCON'S CRY
184—HIDDEN SERPENT
227—FLASHPOINT
262—CUPID'S DAGGER
309—BODYGUARD
366—THE CHARMER
459—FOLLOW ME HOME
487—MYSTERY DAD
574—INNOCENT WITNESS
623—THE MYSTERIOUS TWIN
672—LOST IDENTITY
724—SEMIAUTOMATIC MARRIAGE
792—A DANGEROUS INHERITANCE
840—SHADOWS ON THE LAKE
900—STONEVIEW ESTATE

LOVE INSPIRED
131—ROCKY MOUNTAIN
       MIRACLE
171—HERO IN DISGUISE
194—HIDDEN BLESSING

CAST OF CHARACTERS

Robyn Valcourt—Living in a house of secrets became a terrifying nightmare. She trusted only one man to rescue her.

Brian Donovan—Would his investigation bring justice to a kidnapper and murderer? And when he revealed his identity to Robyn, could she forgive his lies?

Lynette Valcourt—The party for her one-hundred-year-old house sets the scene for disaster.

Heather Fox—The murdered nursemaid whose spirit seems unable to let go of Stoneview Estate.

Nick Bellows—Was he more than a caretaker and friend to the murdered nursemaid, Heather Fox?

Todd Parker—He wanted a deeper romantic relationship with Lynette's beautiful granddaughter, Robyn.

John Parker—Was the influential lawyer responsible for a carefully guarded secret?

Becky Sheldon—A determined young girl with her own agenda.

Chapter One

"Isn't that a grand idea, Robyn? A birthday party for a one-hundred-year-old house?"

Robyn Valcourt searched her sixty-five-year-old grandmother's expression. *She had to be kidding!* "A birthday party, for a house?"

"Why not?" Lynette answered readily. "Houses take on the spirit of the people who live in them. I think it would be fascinating to honor lives that were lived under the same roof."

Robyn wasn't so sure, maybe because she didn't share her grandmother's feelings about Stoneview. Robin hadn't found anything warm and appealing about the old mansion when she'd come to live with her widowed grandmother as a teenager. As a child of parents in the foreign service, Robyn had bounced all over the world, living in one embassy after another. After her parents were killed in a plane crash in southern France, she'd gratefully accepted her grandmother's invitation to come and live with her at Stoneview for her last two years of high school.

The estate encompassed thickly wooded areas and a wide expanse of shoreline along Lake Chataqua, Maine. Historians speculated that an ancient glacier was responsible for digging out the lake bed and scattering enormous boulders near the estate, giving Stoneview its name. In the shadow of tall red oak trees, the mansion stood rather aloof in the center of landscaped grounds sloping down to the water.

From the moment Robyn had stepped through the front door of the house she'd fought a foreboding sense of uneasiness. Large rooms on the main floor were somber and dark, with heavy stone fireplaces and thick-beamed ceilings. A warren of shadowy halls and stairways connected the main floor with the basement, the second floor bedrooms and the attic.

When she was a girl, unseen presences had seemed to lurk in the shadows as Robyn passed through echoing rooms and halls. She imagined muffled, threatening whispers following her as she hurried down the stairs from her bedroom to the warmth of the kitchen and adjoining breakfast room at the back of the house.

Her grandmother's excitement about bringing back the people who had lived there off and on for the last hundred years failed to strike a positive note with Robyn. She pretended an interest in the weird idea that she didn't feel.

Robyn was on spring break from her teaching duties at a private women's college in Portland, Maine. They were sitting on the terrace of her grandmother's winter home in Florida, and Robyn was enjoying the brush of warm, tanning sun upon her winter-pale skin. Hot-pink shorts were a delightful change from her professional wardrobe of tailored suits in subdued shades of green and beige, which toned down the fiery shades of her chestnut hair. They'd been talking about the family mansion, Stoneview, when her grandmother excitedly revealed her latest brainstorm.

"We'll invite members of the families who have lived in the mansion since it was built in 1905. I've already begun the process of tracking down addresses."

Robyn silently sighed. Lynette Valcourt's years as the wife of a foreign diplomat had trained her well. When Robyn's grandfather died shortly after they had retired to Stoneview, Lynette's social life had been sharply curtailed. The vibrant, vivacious woman had been put out to pasture much too early, and it was clear to Robyn that her grandmother had already eagerly begun organizing the whole affair. Her silver-white hair, professionally styled, enhanced her strong features and highlighted dark blue eyes. Lynette's energy level was that of a much younger person, and her tendency to dominate everyone and everything had not faltered during the years.

"We'll try to contact a living descendent of each family, and send out invitations for a centennial birthday celebration," she told Robyn.

"Do you think there will be enough guests to make it all worthwhile?" Robyn asked, playing devil's advocate.

Lynette gave a dismissive wave of her hand. "We'll include special people in the area who have been connected with the estate through the years. Stoneview has been the setting for a good many community projects, you know. People can wander around the place and see what changes have been made to the house and grounds. We can have the affair catered, and arrange for something special like a fireworks display on the lake for the evening.

"We'll ask everyone to bring memorabilia, photos and stories to share," she continued. "Maybe we could even think about writing a history of Stoneview Estate."

The use of the pronoun "we" made it clear Lynette expected her granddaughter to devote time and energy in carrying out the preparations for the affair.

Robyn felt as if she'd been thrust on a runaway train with no way to stop it—or get off! A chill touched her body despite the warm Florida sunshine. *Maybe stirring up the past wasn't such a great idea.* She remembered how the malicious murmuring of high school classmates had ruined the newly decorated bedroom her grandmother had prepared for her arrival.

Her first day, she'd been sitting in the cafeteria with three other girls.

"Really, Robyn, I don't know how you can live in that place after what happened," one of them said with a grimace.

"Doesn't it give you the shivers?" asked another.

"You couldn't pay me enough to have a sleepover there," one girl agreed.

Robyn had looked blankly at the three of them. "What are you talking about?"

Instead of answering, they'd just groaned and rolled their eyes.

When Robyn repeated what they had said to her

grandmother, Lynette dismissed the matter in her usual dogmatic manner.

"This lovely house had four families living in it before your grandfather and I bought it. I'm sure lots of happenings have taken place under this roof, good and bad. The past is past," she had said firmly. "I don't want to hear any more nonsense about it."

Lynette didn't know her granddaughter if she thought that put an end to the matter. As soon as Robyn had the chance, she went to the Chataqua town library. As she scanned the computers of the local *Chataqua Sentinel,* her search paid off. She found what she was looking for.

"Kidnapping and Murder at Stoneview Mansion."

Robyn's breath caught as the headline leaped out at her from the front page. Her heartbeat quickened as she read the account. An adopted infant girl of Darrel and Sybil Sheldon had been snatched from the nursery on the second floor of the Stoneview mansion. After a large ransom had been paid, the baby was left on the doorstep of a local doctor, James Donovan, but that same night, Heather Fox, the nursemaid of the baby, was found murdered on the lawn of the estate. She'd been strangled.

Robyn stared at the photo of a fair-haired young woman, Heather Fox, smiling as she held up a baby for the camera. Robyn could tell from the background that the nursemaid had been standing in front of the garden gazebo, not far from where her body had been discovered. Robyn had shivered as if a cold draft had touched her skin, and wondered if she'd ever be able to pass by that spot again without being reminded of a strangled woman lying there.

"The tragedy has nothing to do with you," Lynette had lectured when Robyn confronted her with the newspaper account. "It's over and done with!"

Robyn had wanted to believe her grandmother, but when they'd stripped the old wallpaper from her bedroom and discovered her room had once been the nursery, the nightmares began. She'd jerk awake in the middle of the night, hearing sounds of a baby crying. Robyn would stare into the shadows, every nerve ending vibrating with an awareness that danger still lurked there. Once, she'd run from the room, trembling, but her grandmother had dismissed her behavior as childish. As a result, Robyn suffered her torment in silence. More than anything she wanted to please her grandmother.

Robyn knew her grandmother's habitual strong Scotch "nightcap" insured her an uneventful, peaceful night's sleep. Although Robin wasn't into drinking as a teenager, one time she'd secretly fixed herself a similar bedtime drink. Her hopes that the liquor would knock her out were foiled even before she consumed half of the glassful. Terribly sick, she'd spent the night in the bathroom, and the next morning had to lie to Lynette about her bedraggled appearance.

Later, when Robyn went away to college and eventually became a professor of romance languages, she was too embarrassed to tell her grandmother that she'd like to change bedrooms when she came back for visits.

Even now, a twenty-six-year-old adult, she hesitated

to express any disapproval of her grandmother's ideas. Appearing to be anything but a confident woman in charge of her own life was out of the question for Robyn. Her parents had expected it—her grandmother demanded it!

"We need to get the invitations sent as soon as possible," Lynette declared, either unaware or totally ignoring her granddaughter's lack of enthusiasm. "By the time I return to Stoneview in June, we should know which families will be staying in the mansion. We can arrange for lodging in Chataqua for the remainder of the guests." She paused. "I think the first week in July would be a perfect time for the celebration, don't you?"

Robyn knew the question was purely rhetorical. As far as her grandmother was concerned the matter was settled. The possibility that she might not be ready and willing to drop all her summer plans and help carry out the festivities wasn't worthy of consideration.

Robyn silently sighed. *No wonder I don't have a life of my own,* she thought. During the school year, the responsibilities of her teaching position demanded total dedication. Every romantic relationship she'd hoped to nurture had died in the bud, smothered by too many other obligations. Several eligible men had shown some interest in dating her, but about the third time she broke a date, it was bye-bye.

"We'll need to mail the invitations as soon as possible," Lynette said as she laid out a timetable for all the preparations.

"Getting current addresses may not be all that easy,"

Robyn protested once again. "What about the descendants of Hugo Koleski, who built the house?"

"Well, several branches of the family lived on the estate until the lumber mill closed in about 1955. I believe that when the property was sold, all the Koleski family moved away."

"Maybe they went back to Poland?"

"We'll have to find out."

"What about the other three owners of Stoneview, before you and Grandpa bought it? How will you track them down?"

"Don't worry. I have friends in high places who have access to public records. I'll make some calls," Lynette assured her, as if that took care of the matter. "After I locate someone in each family, I'll send you the addresses. In the meantime you arrange to have the invitations printed, and be ready to send them out."

"Are you sure about this, Grandmother?" Robyn could not stifle a growing apprehension that such a reunion might dredge up dangerous and conflicting emotions. She didn't know how to explain to her grandmother that on some deep level she sensed there were remaining energies in the house that should be left untouched. Even if she tried to verbalize such intuitive feelings, Robyn knew her grandmother would dismiss them with open disgust.

Sitting there in the warmth of the Florida sun, Robyn sought to deny an insidious warning rippling through her consciousness like the far-off rumble of a deadly storm.

As SHE FINISHED OUT the school year, swamped by the closing demands of her classes and preparations to be away from her town house for the summer, Robyn had little time to think about Stoneview. She was department head of the romance languages department, and the high percentage of foreign students in the small college in Portland, Maine, put extra demands upon her time and energy. Although she found teaching gratifying and was pleased she could put her mastery of languages to good use, she realized she had let her life settle into a tedious routine. But her summer plans to explore some new and untried avenues for her personal development had to be shelved.

The hope that her grandmother would either lose interest in the project or come up short with addresses of the former occupants had been in vain. When the names and addresses arrived, Robyn had indulged herself in a brief period of childish rebellion, and ended up mailing them nearly three weeks later.

As she dropped them into the mailbox, she clung to the hope that her grandmother's brainstorm might somehow be derailed.

Maybe nobody would come.

DETECTIVE BRIAN J. Donovan hated hospitals, especially when the innocent victim of a robbery and assault was an elderly man who had cashed his social security check, then stopped at a sleazy pool hall and bar to have a drink. A couple of druggies had waited for him, beaten him up and left him unconscious in the alley.

Police files were filled with such cases. Brian knew the chances of getting any solid leads from the victim were slight. At the age of twenty-eight, he'd seen enough selfish brutality to last a lifetime. There was an angry stiffness about him as he strode up to the hospital admittance desk.

"Evening, Detective." The pretty nurse smiled as her appreciative glance passed over his tawny hair, brown eyes and athletic build. "You're out late. The sun will be up in a few hours." Her voice took on a flirtatious tone. "If you're still around, I might offer to fix you some breakfast."

Brian smiled, recognizing the intimacy in her invitation, but he'd learned to maneuver around such overtures, especially on the job. "I'll take a rain check," he answered lightly.

"Promises, promises," she said, sighing. "What can I do for you tonight?"

Brian glanced at his notebook. "An elderly man, Joseph Keller, was brought in about eleven o'clock. Assault and battery."

After checking her computer, she nodded. "Room 209. Condition stable."

"That's good. Thanks." Brian knew the first few hours after an incident were the most productive in getting a line on criminal perpetrators. After that, imagination often took over and filled in the gaps. He reached the room just as a male nurse was coming out.

Brian flashed his badge. "Detective Donovan. Any chance I can spend a couple of minutes with Mr. Keller?"

"I just gave him a sedative, so you'd better make it fast," the young man warned. "He's beat up pretty bad. A tough old guy. Fought the thugs off pretty good, but they got his wallet."

"Any other personal effects?" Brian asked. "Forensics might be able to get some fingerprints if the muggers went through his pockets."

"He didn't have much. There are a few things in the bedside drawer."

"Thanks." Brian eased inside the room and approached the bed quietly. "Mr. Keller?"

Even though the man's prone body clearly showed his advanced age, there was a sharpness in his glare. Dark eyes in a bruised and scratched face narrowed as he stared at Brian. His voice was raspy and breathless as he croaked, "What the hell do you want?"

"We want to find the thugs who did this to you. I'm Detective Donovan."

"You get my money back?"

"We're going to try our best, Mr. Keller. Can you tell me what happened?"

He closed his eyes for a long moment and then looked at Brian as the words came painfully slow. "The bastards came up from behind. Dragged me into the alley. Went through my pockets. Knocked me out."

"Can you tell me what they looked like?"

The Adam's apple in his skinny throat bobbed as he swallowed hard. "Hoodlums. Young and white. Too dark to see much."

Brian closed his notebook. Unfortunately, the old man's description was too generic to be of value. "If you remember anything else, Mr. Keller, just call me." He laid his card on the bedside table. "You take care of yourself."

"If I'd been younger I'd have shown them a thing or

two," he rasped, and his slack jaw tightened a little. "Was a heavyweight boxer in my prime."

"Really?" Brian smiled at the old man. "How about that?"

"Plenty of money and women, too." He gave Brian a grin. "Owned the biggest estate on Lake Chataqua."

"Lake Chataqua, Maine?" Brian's eyes narrowed.

"Yep. Owned the Stoneview Estate, I did. You know it?"

"Yes, my father had a medical practice in Chataqua until I was almost seventeen, and we moved to Boston."

Just the name Stoneview instantly brought a hot anger surging through Brian. His father's professional reputation had been ruined by a kidnapping and murder that had taken place at the estate during Brian's senior year in high school. As the family doctor for Darrel and Sybil Sheldon, his dad had attended their newly adopted baby and the ill-fated nursemaid, Heather Fox. When the missing baby showed up on Dr. Donovan's doorstep, and the nursemaid he'd befriended was found strangled, ugly speculations had targeted Brian's father as a likely accomplice. The police failed to turn up any leads to the ransom money or the parties responsible for the nanny's death.

When insidious suspicions destroyed his father's reputation and the town turned against him, Brian had felt the backlash in his own life. His father decided to uproot the family, and in the move, Brian had lost touch with all his high school friends. His boyhood had been a happy one, living in the house where he'd been born, hanging out with his buddies and growing up with a sense of belonging. He'd never recovered from the isolation of the move, and had tried to protect himself from that kind of loss ever again by becoming pretty much a loner.

"You must have heard of me," the injured man insisted. "Heavyweight boxer? Made big money, I did."

Joe Keller. Suddenly, the name snagged a memory. Brian remembered that a lawyer friend of his father, John Parker, had bought the Stoneview Estate cheap from a prizefighter whose career had hit the skids. Before Joe Keller had sold it, he'd rented the place out as a questionable resort until the authorities closed it down for suspected gambling. Obviously, the fighter's good fortune had gone downhill since then. Brian found it hard to believe this wasted old man had once been a force in the boxing ring.

"What about your family, Joe?" Brian asked. "Have the authorities notified anyone about what happened to you tonight?"

"No one to notify," he answered in a tight voice.

Brian checked the bedside drawer, which the nurse had said contained Joe's personal effects: a pitiful pile of change, a lighter, half pack of cigarettes and a white envelope. Not much to go on.

"If anyone handled any of these things besides you, we may be able to match some fingerprints," Brian told him hopefully.

"Just mail that envelope for me," Joe said tiredly. "Tell 'em I'm not up to that kind of shindig. It's an invitation. A hundred-year-old birthday party for a house. Doesn't that beat all?"

Brian didn't answer. He removed the invitation and bagged the envelope with everything else. After leaving the hospital, he drove to his small apartment in a modest Boston neighborhood. Since most of his time was spent on the job, or working out at a nearby gym, the apartment was hardly more than a place to sleep and eat. Occasionally he enjoyed feminine company, but never for very long.

His telephone was blinking with a couple of messages. The only personal one was from his mother, asking him to call. His parents had moved to sunny New Mexico several years earlier after his father had retired from medical practice. The dark cloud that had forced Dr. Donovan to give up his practice in Chataqua had never dissipated. The unsolved kidnapping and murder seemed to lodge in the doctor's mind like a curse, and even moving across the country had not seemed to help.

Brian returned his mother's call, and she told him that she was really worried about his dad. "Nothing seems to be physically wrong, but he's slipping into a deep despondency and brooding about the past. He's dredging up everything that happened in Chataqua." Her voice wavered. "It breaks my heart."

"I know, Mom. He probably has too much time on his hands."

"He's not interested in making new friends or taking up a new hobby. You know how stubborn he can be."

Brian tried to console her as much as he could, but there was very little comfort he could give her. It was a damn shame that what had happened eleven years ago could still destroy the last few years of his father's life.

Too keyed up to sleep, Brian slumped down in his chair, sipping a beer and staring out the window. His thoughts centered on the unexpected encounter with Joseph Keller, and the invitation the boxer had received. What kind of nonsense was that? A birthday party for a damn house!

Even as Brian dismissed the idea, a startling possibility presented itself. The urge to investigate the crimes that had cast suspicion on his father had always been at the back of Brian's mind during his career as a detective. As long as the matter remained in Cold Case files, Brian knew no one was going to spend any time or energy on it. As he thought about the invitation that had come into his possession, he began to realize he'd been handed a viable undercover identity.

Joseph Keller wouldn't be attending the celebration at the Stoneview estate, and no one would be going to represent him. Brian could accept the invitation as a distant relative of Joe Keller.

For a welcomed guest at the Stoneview mansion, Brian knew, on-the-spot investigation would be possible. Attending the event would be invaluable, not only because of access to the crime scene, but because of contact with people who might have pertinent information that had gone unnoticed when the crimes occurred.

He knew he'd never get official approval. The department was stretched just covering day-to-day investigations. This undercover job would have to be done in secret and on his own. He had vacation time coming, and the opportunity to spend it at Stoneview was worth the gamble. He checked the calendar. The celebration was less than three weeks away, and he ought to be able to get free from his duties ten days before that.

As Brian weighed the deception from all perspectives, the advantages made his decision an easy one. His mother had pleaded with him to do something to help, and what better thing could he do than try and clear his father's name once and for all?

He decided to wait until the next morning before making a decision, but the idea was only more firmly planted in his mind the next day.

He read the invitation again carefully, filled in the requested information and boldly identified himself as a distant relative of Joseph Keller. In a place for comments, he expressed his pleasure in representing the Keller family at the "one-hundred-year-old birthday celebration."

With deliberate deception, he signed his name "Brian Keller." In most undercover situations it was better to use a familiar first name than to suddenly try to relate to a brand-new one, he knew. Besides, most people in Chataqua had known him as Buddy Donovan during his school days.

Brian sealed the envelope, affixed the proper postage, and early the next morning mailed the RSVP to a Ms. Robyn Valcourt at the designated return address.

Finally, he'd get the answers he sought—no matter what.

Chapter Two

Brian arrived in Chataqua a little more than a week before the festivities at Stoneview were scheduled. The bustling small town hugged the northern side of a large lake, and impressive homes like Stoneview overlooked the water on the opposite side. Brian had been on Chataqua Lake numerous times when he was growing up, but he'd never set foot on the exclusive Stoneview property.

He wandered briefly around the town, visiting familiar places of his childhood. Brian remembered his disappointment at having to move away just as his high school baseball team was competing for the state championship. He'd helped bring home a regional trophy the year before, and had never replaced the friendships or sense of belonging in the unfamiliar Boston school where he'd graduated.

When he met people in the bustling resort town he'd known in his youth, he gave them every chance to challenge his assumed identity. None did. Brian wasn't surprised. He'd been called Buddy Donovan instead of Brian. He'd been a tall, skinny, sun-bleached-blond

teenager when he'd moved away. He was still tall—six
feet—but training at the police academy had totally
changed his physique. His face had filled out, and a recent
dye job had turned his hair a dark brown. He was fairly
confident that he could engage in his undercover investigation without worrying about recognition. His father
was the one who had known the Sheldons and Heather
Fox, the murdered nursemaid. In the years he'd been
away, Brian had never had any social contact with the
families of past or present residents of the Stoneview
estate.

After mailing the invitation response to Robyn
Valcourt, Brian had learned she was Lynette Valcourt's
granddaughter, an unmarried professor of romance languages at an exclusive women's college in Portland. A
child of parents in the diplomatic service, she'd come
to live at Stoneview two years after Brian's family had
left Chataqua, so they had never met. Brian pictured her
as very staid, distant and bookish, a product of a class-
conscious society.

In preparing for his undercover deception, he'd pored
over every scrap of information recorded in the police
files at the time of the crimes. He went over and over
every detail, trying to come to terms with one inconsist-
ency that kept nagging at him. The timing of the nursemaid's murder seemed wrong. Heather Fox had not
been killed the night the baby was snatched, as would
be expected if she was trying to protect her charge.
Instead, the ransom had been paid and the baby returned
when the nursemaid was found strangled on the estate
grounds a day later. Why then and not earlier?

More than ever, he was determined to use this unexpected opportunity to conduct his own "on site" investigation, and clear his father's reputation once and for all.
His agenda was to interact with the people who had been
involved, and follow up any clues that came to light or
might have been missed in the original investigation.
Since he had no idea of the current situation at Stoneview, he'd have to play it by ear and hope for the best.

Instead of renting a car in Chataqua, he decided to
approach Stoneview by water in a small rented motorboat. It was midafternoon when he steered it across
Chataqua Lake toward the large white mansion built on
a slight rise on the opposite shore. Landscaped lawns
and gardens were bordered by thick forested areas that
provided a natural privacy for the estate, isolating it
from other homes on that side of the lake. As he came
closer, Brian saw two people standing near the boathouse and cement pier.

Good, he thought. *This might make things easier.*

He wasn't looking forward to walking up to the
house and presenting himself, cold turkey, at the door.
As he cut the motor and eased the craft toward the dock,
both the man and woman turned around, watching him.

A muscular, middle-aged fellow in workman's
clothes peered at Brian pugnaciously from under the
brim of his straw hat. The bullish air about him didn't
invite unexpected social calls, and the young woman
beside him seemed equally guarded. She must have been
in her early twenties, Brian guessed. Her hair was the
color of reddish-brown fall leaves, and she was wearing
pale green slacks that hugged her shapely figure.

Could this be the granddaughter?

Brian's preconceived idea of a bookish college professor took an instant dive. Such an appealing feminine body and delicate features certainly didn't match the mental picture he'd had. Still, there was something about the way she held herself that warned him she was, indeed, Robyn Valcourt. He had the impression from their body language that she'd been instructing the man about some task.

Brian offered a friendly wave as he walked toward them, and without waiting for any response, quickly introduced himself.

"Hi, I'm Brian Keller. My great-uncle is Joseph Keller. I responded to an invitation to the birthday celebration," he added. "Regretfully, Joe is too ill to come."

"Joe Keller, the fighter!" The man's ruddy face lost its glower as he broke into a wide smile. He looked to be somewhere in his early forties, with sandy hair, bushy eyebrows and ruddy features. "Well, I'll be. My dad was one of Joe Keller's biggest fans. Pa was working at one of the neighboring estates when Keller lived here. They were about the same age. He won a pile of money on Joe's fights. Lost a pile, too," he admitted with an even broader smile.

"Is that so?" Brian laughed with him.

The man stuck out a callused hand. "Nick Bellows."

"Nice to meet you, Nick. I'll have to tell Joe about his secret admirer."

There was nothing of Nick's open-armed friendliness in Robyn Valcourt's manner when Nick introduced her as "Miss Valcourt." She simply nodded and gave him a cool, "Hello."

Even though she was better looking than Brian had imagined, her distant manner didn't surprise him. Obviously, his inopportune arrival had put her on guard.

"It's a pleasure to meet you, Ms. Valcourt," he responded politely. "I've been looking forward to visiting Stoneview."

"And you'll be coming back for the celebration, Mr. Keller?" she asked politely, but in a tone that clearly emphasized the affair was more than a week away.

"Yes, of course." Brian glanced innocently toward the house, which was approached by a long red cement sidewalk from the water's edge. "Joe has some very fond memories of this place. I was hoping you might not mind if I had a look around before the busy day."

"We're on a tight schedule," she answered quickly.

"I understand. A big event like this must take a lot of planning."

She gave him a fleeting smile as if she appreciated his recognition of the hard work that went into a centennial celebration.

"We've got plenty to do before then," Nick agreed as he waved an exasperated hand toward a two-story boathouse, where large doors had fallen inward and crushed the two boats inside. "Look at that, would you?"

"Wow, what happened?" Brian asked, hoping to keep the conversation going while he figured out how to get past Miss Robyn Valcourt's resistance.

"A blasted ice storm last winter!" Nick swore. "Strong winds whipped everything in sight. All the custom-made repair parts have finally arrived. Tore the boathouse doors right off their hinges. Don't know how I can get it ready in time." He directed this last sentence to Robyn, and added, "You'll have to explain to your grandmother that I'm not a miracle worker—especially with all the other stuff I've got to do."

"Maybe I could help out some way?" Brian suggested smoothly. "My plans are to just hang around Chataqua, waiting for the big day. My dad and I built a cabin a couple of summers ago. I learned to use a hammer and saw pretty good. I'd be glad to have something to do."

Nick raised a questioning eyebrow at Robyn. "Sounds good to me."

"We wouldn't want to impose," Robyn said smoothly, a firm dismissal in her tone.

"I wouldn't have offered if that were the case." Brian gave her his best people-management smile.

"What kind of business are you in, Mr. Keller?"

"Oh, I have my fingers in quite a few projects. I'm an independent business analyst—on vacation."

"He could bunk with me in the cottage," Nick suggested. "We've got that extra room, and you were just saying that we might have an overflow from the house."

"I don't know, Mr. Keller—"

"Brian," he quickly corrected.

The way her blue eyes, clear and deep as a summer sky, measured him, he knew he'd made a mistake moving into familiarity so soon. He'd have to be more careful. Undoubtedly, she was used to fending off people.

She turned to Nick. "Grandmother is planning a fire-works display on the lake in the evening. Getting the boathouse in shape is a priority."

"Along with a dozen others," Nick muttered.

"I know."

"With an extra hand, it's more likely to get ready in time. I'm not even sure I could manage clearing out the debris by myself," Nick insisted.

"All right, then. We accept your offer, Mr. Keller. If you don't have other plans?"

"No, my time is my own," he assured her. "Spending a few days at Stoneview will be more than a pleasure."

As ROBYN LEFT THE MEN and started walking up the long sidewalk to the house, she could feel them watching her. She kept her head up and her carriage straight. If Nick hadn't been running on overload, she wouldn't have even considered accepting the offer of this stranger. With a dozen "have-to-dos" in the house and grounds waiting for his attention, an extra pair of hands would be a godsend. Her grandmother would have a fit about letting a guest move in with them more than a week before the party, but Lynette wasn't in charge, Robyn reminded herself.

For weeks, her grandmother had been making plans and giving orders—from a distance, of course. At the moment, Lynette was in the Bahamas. She had decided at the last minute to attend a "divine socialite wedding-of-the-year" that she vowed "just couldn't be missed."

Even Lynette's loyal hired cook and housekeeper, Olga Dietz, was rebelling at all the extra work. She was a sturdy German woman in her forties who had been with Robyn's grandparents since their duties at the German embassy almost twenty years ago. Her husband had died before the Valcourts moved to Stoneview. Mrs. Dietz had never quite become "Americanized," and her stubborn manner kept Lynette from trying to dictate how to run the kitchen and supervise the day help.

Every telephone call from Lynette brought more instructions about engaging the right caterers, photographers, florists, entertainers, and getting the house and grounds in perfect condition.

It wasn't as if she couldn't handle the responsibility, Robyn reminded herself. She could. She knew it, and her grandmother knew it. But the truth was that at some deep level she was utterly sick and tired of being reliable, capable and dependable. Robyn longed to get in her car and head north to the oceanside resort where she'd planned to spend her summer vacation. But even as the desire crossed her mind, she knew she'd never do it. Such irresponsible action would be unthinkable. What she didn't need was an early guest to complicate matters. Under different conditions she might have been more hospitable, but at the moment she wasn't in the mood to handle any unexpected demands. Already she was having second thoughts about agreeing to accept Brian Keller's help.

On some intuitive level, she sensed he was going to be a disruptive force. His manner seemed sincere, but there had been a pure masculine energy about him that she didn't trust. His clinging white T-shirt accented the breadth and hardness of his chest, and tight jeans followed the shape of his long muscular legs. Dark brown hair was nicely layered, and everything about him seemed calculated to impress any female within a fifty-mile radius. Robyn chided herself for even noticing.

She purposefully made her way through the dark halls of the house to the library. After sitting down at a massive walnut desk, she turned on the computer to view the full agenda waiting for her attention, and put Brian Keller firmly out of her mind....

NICK AND BRIAN WORKED well together. They were both tired and sweaty when they climbed a circular iron staircase to the second floor of the boathouse, which had been made into a recreation room, complete with comfortable furniture and a refreshment bar. Fortunately, the devastation of the winter ice storm last January had been confined to the lower level, and the party room had been spared.

"When the Valcourts bought the house from the Sheldons, this was a workout room with exercise equipment, and they remodeled it into a party room. I liked it better the other way," Nick told him as he walked over to a small refrigerator. "Beer or water?"

"Water, thanks."

"Beer for me."

He handed Brian a bottle of water and popped the cap on his beer. After taking a deep swig, he dropped down in a large leather chair opposite the couch where Brian was sitting.

"How long have you been at Stoneview, Nick?" Brian asked in a relaxed, chatty tone.

"Too long," he answered bluntly as he lit a cigarette. "I came here with the Sheldons when they bought the estate, mainly because I'd been their caretaker at their previous home. And when they up and sold Stoneview, I decided to stay on and work for the Valcourts. I like the cottage and the lake, and most of the year there's not much that has to be done. It's a pretty neat place to live."

"You must feel kind of possessive of it."

"I guess ruts get comfortable after awhile," he admitted. "And I like having the run of the place. Old lady Valcourt travels a lot, and the granddaughter has her own town house where she teaches. The Sheldons were easy to work for, too."

"So you were here at Stoneview when the unfortunate tragedy happened?" Brian asked casually, hoping he wasn't moving too fast. The fact that Nick had brought up the topic of the Sheldons was a welcome surprise. It gave him hope that if Nick was in a reminiscing mood, he might share some valuable on-the-scene insights that didn't get into the police reports.

"Oh, you heard about that, did you? Yep, I was here." Nick nearly emptied his bottle of beer before he added, "The police were all over the place. Asked a lot of questions, but, hell, I didn't have anything to tell them. I've never made it my business to know what goes on in the big house. Not with the Sheldons. Not with the Valcourts. I keep to myself." Nick drank more of his beer. "I couldn't tell them anything."

Or wouldn't? Brian wondered silently. Something about Nick's denial rang false. He'd bet anything that little got past those sharp eyes of his. Before Brian could come up with a comment that might encourage more confidences, Nick changed the subject. Brian had to content himself with waiting for another time when, perhaps, Nick had more beer under his belt.

"We can't do much more until I check the lumber-yard, and order more material and hardware." Nick finished off his beer. "Let's call it a day."

Brian nodded in agreement, and as they made their way out of the boathouse, he told Nick, "I have a backpack and small bag in the boat. I was thinking about spending a few days at one of those resorts on the lake, but this is a whole lot better."

Nick seemed to accept the explanation without question. After Brian retrieved his bags, they made their way around the house to a small cottage at the back of property where a wooded area met an access road. A curved driveway led past the small house to a four-car garage, and a tree-lined walk led to the back door of the mansion. Another wide sidewalk circled the house to the front entrance.

As Nick opened the cottage door, he waved Brian inside. "Home sweet home. You'll have to excuse the mess."

Brian could see what Nick meant—a neat house-keeper he was not! The small living room opening off of the front hall showed signs of careless bachelor living. Clutter was everywhere. Books, cups, newspa-pers and a few discarded pieces of clothing were scat-tered about on the furniture and floor.

Nick chuckled, a bit red with embarrassment as Brian surveyed the room. "Didn't know I was going to have company."

"Not company," Brian assured him.

"Well, I haven't had much of that," Nick admitted. "Kinda like it that way. I was never one to need a bunch of people around. Me and my Siamese cat are loners, although I think lusty Sinbad has sired more than his share of litters." He laughed. "I swear, every house up and down the lake has a Siamese cat or two sunning on the doorstep."

Even as he spoke, a large, beautifully colored seal point Siamese sauntered in from the kitchen and rubbed against Nick's legs.

"I know, it's chow time, old fellow," Nick said affectionately. "He's eleven years old, would you believe? Heather, the nursemaid, got him when he was a kitten and after she was killed, he disappeared for a while. About six months later, I found Sinbad on my doorstep. He's been with me ever since. I think Heather would like it that way."

There hadn't been much in the police reports about the murdered nursemaid. Maybe Nick would fill out the picture a little? "Were you and Heather friends?"

"Just employees of the same family. The house staff kept pretty much to themselves."

"Why is that?"

He shrugged. "Who knows? I suppose the owners wanted it that way. Come on, I'll show you where to bunk."

There were two small bedrooms on the second floor and a nice-sized bathroom. The clutter visible through the open door of the front bedroom made it obvious that it was Nick's,

In contrast, the back bedroom was clean, neat and

rather sterile, like a motel room. Brian was pleased to see he had a good view of the back of the mansion in case he needed to do some night prowling to check out the premises.

"Why don't you hit the shower first, Brian, and I'll get something going for supper?"

"Sounds good."

"You may change your mind when you taste my cooking." He turned to leave, and then stopped. "Oh, by the way, after dinner I'm supposed to bring chairs down from the attic and set them up in the basement recreation room. The old lady wants to set up a kinda cabaret down there. How about giving me a hand?"

"Sure, be glad to help," Brian offered readily.

Perfect! He wanted to make use of every chance he got to familiarize himself with every inch of the house and grounds. All in all, the situation was better than he'd anticipated. He had the opening he needed to the premises, and he intended to take full advantage of it.

As he quickly showered and changed into a pair of brown corduroys and an open-neck sports shirt, his thoughts centered on the attractive Robyn Valcourt and the obstacle she might be in his investigation. Obviously, she wasn't the kind to give him free run of the house. Keeping her from being suspicious of his deception might be his greatest challenge.

For supper, Nick fixed a simple meal of eggs, fried potatoes and steak. The kitchen was surprisingly orderly and clean compared to the living room and the glimpse Brian had had of Nick's bedroom. The two men ate in companionable silence. Sinbad threaded their legs with hopeful anticipation, even though he'd already consumed his can of food. Nick fondly nudged him away and scolded him for being such a moocher.

After they'd cleared the table and stacked dishes in a small dishwasher, Nick said, "We'd better get a move on. I'd like to get to bed before midnight."

They entered the house through the back door, and as if Nick knew where to find Robyn this time of evening, he led the way down a wide, echoing hall until they came to double doors opening into the library. Most of the room was in shadows except for one far corner, where a radius of light highlighted a large desk.

Robyn was sitting at a computer, and from a half-eaten sandwich and a drink on the desk beside her, Brian suspected she'd had her dinner on a tray.

She gave the men a questioning glance, and quickly finished the entry she'd been making before greeting them with a lift of her reddish-brown eyebrows.

"Brian's volunteered to help me collect chairs for the recreation room," Nick told her.

"Oh?" She studied Brian in a calculating, measuring way, as if suspicious of his Good Samaritan role.

He couldn't blame her. She must be used to hangers-on trying to manipulate her and her money. He applauded her caution. In police work he dealt with too many victims who failed to be wary when it came to strangers invading their lives.

He felt a little guilty as he lied, "Joe would want me to help out. He has fond memories of this house, and I know he's going to love hearing about it. I bet there's been a lot a changes in it since he lived here."

Robyn's forehead smoothed slightly. "I'm sorry he isn't well enough to come. Maybe we can telephone him and let a few people say hello to him?"

Was her suggestion an innocent or a calculating one? Had she already become suspicious of his premature arrival?

Brian knew that if this smart lady really put her mind to it, tracking down Joe Keller in the hospital or nursing home wouldn't be all that difficult.

"I'll certainly tell him people asked about him," Brian said, sidestepping her suggestion.

"Well, let's get on it," Nick urged. "I knew we should have stored the extra chairs in the basement. I told Mrs. Valcourt lugging them up and down from the attic was a waste of time."

"I agree, Nick. Grandmother got used to having a lot of paid help when she lived abroad."

"Well, turning the rec room into a cabaret for one evening is going to demand a lot of extra work."

"I know. If the boathouse is usable, some of the crowd will head there for drinks and dancing, but others will probably stay downstairs in the rec room." She turned off the computer and rose to her feet. "I'll check the arrangement of the tables while you bring down the chairs."

"Why don't you leave some of that for the extra hired help?" Nick frowned. "When are they coming?"

"Two days before the affair. Grandmother thought that would be early enough."

Nick grumbled something inaudible.

"I know." Robyn smiled at him. "That's what you

get for working miracles every time she comes up with one of her ideas, Nick. She knows you'll come through for her."

"Maybe not this time," he threatened, but there was little conviction in his tone. "Well, come on, Brian, let's get at it."

The stairway to the attic opened off of the back hall and rose to a third floor that spanned the width of the house. At one end was an enclosed storeroom, apparently filled with items like folding chairs that were used from time to time.

The rest of the attic looked like a garage sale gone berserk. Barrels, trunks, metal lockers, pictures, stored furniture and miscellaneous discards of all kinds covered every inch of floor space.

Was this the accumulation from all the five families who had lived in the house? Brian wondered. The nursery and nanny's room had probably been stripped before the Valcounts bought the house. Were any of Heather's personal effects stored in the boxes that were stacked throughout the attic?

Brian wanted to question Nick about the possibility, but he knew he had to wait. Rushing things could land him out of the house on his ear. He mentally made a note to make a personal search of the attic at the first safe opportunity.

As they started bringing chairs down to the basement, Brian was surprised at the spaciousness of the recreation room. Not only was there a full bar, but a nice-size dance floor, complete with a large jukebox that would have made any antique dealer drool.

"Does it still work?" Brian asked, peering at the layered 78 rpm records.

He was startled when Robyn unexpectedly came up behind him and plugged in a cord. Instantly, the machine glowed with gaudy colors and blinking lights. As she touched a selection, one of the 78 rpm records dropped smoothly into place.

He laughed when the bouncy notes of "Chattanooga Choo Choo" filled the room. Robyn swayed slightly in rhythm with the music, and he was startled by the relaxed sweetness of her mouth and the dreamy softness in her eyes. Soft wisps of gingery hair highlighted her smooth complexion, and long seductive curls caressed her cheeks. One thing he knew for certain—every ounce of Robyn Valcourt's supple body was aching to dance!

Boldly, he reached out, took her hands and twirled her in a complete spin before she had a chance to protest. He eased her into position and grinned at her. "Shall we dance?"

Without giving her an option, he quickly initiated some easy jitterbug steps. Not only did she follow him, but even challenged him to match some intricate patterns of her own. She threw back her head and laughed at his expression of surprise. By the time the record ended, both of them were breathing heavily and laughing.

Nick shook his head. He'd been watching them with an expression of disbelief on his face. "What is it with you two?" he chided impatiently. "Are we going to get this place ready or not?"

Brian watched Robyn's countenance suddenly lose

its effervescence. Tense lines immediately replaced the smile curves around her lips. She looked a little like a child who'd been caught shirking her duties. He wanted to say something, but didn't know what might be appropriate. He couldn't take a chance on ruining this unexpected connection with her.

"What about it, Brian?" Nick demanded. "Are you going to help or not?"

"Sure thing," he answered smoothly. He wondered if Nick's irritation was really about work, or if he was jealous of Robyn's attention. "Thanks for the dance," he told her, and then turned to follow Nick up the stairs.

ROBYN HAD LEARNED dances of different kinds the year her parents were stationed in France. Embassy kids attending the same school had access to a jukebox and indulged in a lot of impromptu parties. Unfortunately, after Robyn came to live with her grandmother her social life had not included many dances. In secret, she'd enjoyed the private pleasure of spending time in the rec room, playing the jukebox and dancing by herself.

As she caught her breath, she realized what a delight it was to be actually dancing with a smooth, easy-moving partner whose gentle but firm touch guided her with such persuasion. When he'd twirled her away from him in a dizzying spin, and then brought her back to him, she'd let herself lean shamelessly against him. She had abandoned herself to the joy of the music and the harmony of their bodies moving together.

Nick's critical remarks had quickly dissipated the

release and exuberance she'd felt while dancing. As she caught her breath, she realized that it might be a little embarrassing to be around Brian Keller after what had happened.

"I need some air," she said as she brushed back some moist hair clinging to her forehead.

The sky was slightly overcast as she left the house by the main door. Clouds passing in front of the moon sent flickering shadows through branches of tall oak trees and across the lawn. The quiet seclusion of the vine-covered gazebo beckoned her. Sitting down on one of the small benches, she kept going over in her mind the disturbing way she'd reacted to Brian Keller.

It was the darn music. That's what had made her forget herself. She certainly hadn't been trying to make time with Joe Keller's relative. Even now she flushed, remembering the intimate way he had smiled at her. He must have known how much she enjoyed dancing with him. Had he deliberately exploited the situation? Something about him just didn't ring true. She wanted to know a lot more about him before she let herself accept Brian Keller at face value. He was too damn sexy. *And I'm too damn lonely.*

The admission was lost when her ears suddenly were assaulted by a high-pitched wailing. The noise was too abrasive for an infant's cry, and yet that's what it resembled.

What on earth…? Cautiously, she stepped out of the gazebo. As her gaze swept the expanse of lawn and nearby landscaped areas, she couldn't see anything that might be responsible for the strange cry.

She stiffened as she remembered the newspaper photo of the murdered nursemaid standing in front of the gazebo, holding the kidnapped baby, in about this very spot.

Robyn waited for the spine-tingling sound to come again, and when it did, she forced herself to turn in that direction. She caught a flicker of movement in a nearby landscape planting of shrubs, trees and rocks.

As she came closer, two baby-blue eyes stared at her out of the darkness. At the same moment, wailing that could have been an infant's cry filled her ears again. She froze and then backed up as a rustling in the middle of the planting increased. Her breath caught when a shadowy form took shape.

Then she laughed in embarrassment. The blue eyes belonged to Nick's old cat. She hadn't seen him around the last few times she'd been at Stoneview.

The Siamese must be about eleven years old now, Robyn thought as he began stroking her legs with his sleek, arched back. She bent down and petted him.

"What's the matter, old fellow? What are you doing, wandering around and wailing? Chasing away evil spirits?"

Even as the words left her mouth, she wished them back.

The cat had been lying in the same spot where Heather's body had been found. Was his high-pitched wailing for the mistress that had been slain there?

Chapter Three

A clock somewhere in the cottage chimed midnight as Brian stood looking out the bedroom window. Against the night sky, the spacious mansion rose dark and imposing. A capricious moon shining through scattered clouds created an uncertain glow on the shadowy grounds as tree branches moved fitfully in a taunting wind. Brian heard the lake water lashing relentlessly against the shore, creating a restless mood that matched his feelings.

He wasn't at all pleased about what had happened that evening. Dancing with Miss Robyn Valcourt had been a mistake. A big one! Her guard had gone up the minute the music had ended. She obviously felt uncomfortable over what had happened. Too late, he realized that dancing with her in such an impulsive way had somehow threatened her. Now more than ever, she might be less tolerant, and more suspicious of his casual arrival.

Brian wished he could have been able to use an identity more circumspect than a relative of Joe Keller.

The fighter's reputation had made for good tabloid news. Joe had played around plenty, and earned a reputation of being fast and free with women. Whether true or false, rumors of crooked fights and illegal gambling had followed him. Undoubtedly, Nick knew about the bad press, and a person as perceptive as Robyn might start questioning the unexpected arrival of someone related to him. What was Brian Keller really after? she might wonder. A good time? Or something else?

Brian sighed as he turned away from the window and threw himself down on the narrow bed. No doubt about it, he'd have to be more careful. Staying undercover was a must. He couldn't jeopardize his investigation. If anyone tumbled to his real motive there would be little chance of bringing forth any new evidence. Avoiding any kind of personal familiarity with Robyn Valcourt was advisable.

Even as Brian resolved to keep his distance from her, the memory of her feminine softness in the circle of his arms taunted him. A dangerous impulse to challenge the wild, untethered spirit behind that formal facade of hers had been born when he'd caught a glimpse of the real Robyn Valcourt.

SHE WAS JUST COMING DOWN the stairs the next morning when the front doorbell rang. Who could that be? None of the service people would be using the front entrance. She was slightly frowning when she opened the door to a beaming, round-faced woman with uncertain blondish-gray hair, and a chubby girl about eleven years old.

"Hi, Robyn." Melva Sheldon greeted her with a wide smile.

"Surprise!" piped the girl.

Robyn's stomach tightened. *No, it couldn't be. Not two more early guests. Melva Sheldon and her grand-daughter, Becky.*

Even though Darrel and Sybil Sheldon had bought a home just across the lake after selling Stoneview, they rarely came back for a visit, undoubtedly because of the unpleasantness of the kidnapping and murder. But Darrel's mother, Melva, who lived with them, had become close friends with Lynette. Both women were in their sixties, and widows, and Melva had been to Stoneview quite frequently.

Somehow, Robyn found her voice and her manners. "How nice to see you both. Please come in."

Becky bounced into the house without hesitation. Her blue eyes were alert and held a glint of curiosity as she looked around. Dark curly hair was caught in a red ribbon that matched her polka-dotted shorts and top. Robyn hadn't seen Becky since she was about two years old.

"Your grandmother called me, Robyn," Melva explained. "And asked me to come a few days early—"

"So here we are!" Becky grinned broadly. "We're here to help you."

Robyn fought to keep a smile on her face as she silently fumed. Just like Lynette to ease her own conscience by drafting someone else to carry out her orders.

"That's very kind of you, but—" Robyn began.

"Now don't argue," Melva said firmly. "Lynette

warned me that you'd refuse the offer. But it's all settled. I was just babysitting Becky, waiting for her parents to get back in a couple of days from a trip, anyway. I might as well be here, helping out."

"And me, too," Becky added as she held up a small cardboard suitcase. "I have everything I need to do my job."

Puzzled, Robyn asked, "And what job is that, Becky?"

Her eyes sparkled. "Didn't you know I was the baby kidnapped from this very house? It was in the newspapers and everything," she bragged, obviously proud of her public notoriety.

"Of course she knew," Melva said firmly. "But we don't want to talk about it, Becky."

"If nobody talks about it, I won't have anything to put in my detective notebook," she wailed.

"Oh, dear." Melva sighed and sent Robyn an apologetic look. "Becky, we'll talk about this later." She gave her granddaughter a "please, not now" glance that Becky ignored.

"I have everything I need in here. See? It's a sleuth kit for young detectives. That's me," she said proudly. "I can take fingerprints, shoot pictures, write down what people say, and there's even a small recorder."

Robyn silently groaned. *This isn't happening.*

"You can't be a pest, Becky," her grandmother warned. "It's all right to play your little games, but you have to stay out of people's way."

"Okay, Grammie," Becky agreed happily, and then gave Robyn a wide grin. "Where's the nursery? I'm supposed to make some sketches."

"Nursery? But—"

"Yes, the scene of the crime. That's where you start, you know. And look for clues."

"Rebecca Sheldon, that's absolutely enough," her grandmother said firmly. "Now, let's decide what needs to be done first. Someone can bring in our luggage later." She slipped her plump arm through Robyn's. "You don't look very perky to me. How have you been sleeping? It's a good thing Lynette called me. I bet you haven't been eating. Have you had breakfast?"

"I'm hungry," Becky announced. "Do you have any creamy chocolate bars?"

"I don't think so," Robyn answered in a far-off voice that didn't sound like her own, as they headed down the hall to a small breakfast room off the kitchen.

Mrs. Dietz was setting out coffee for Robyn, and her strong German face broke into a wreath of smiles when she saw Melva Sheldon.

"You're a bit early for the goings-on," the housekeeper chided with mock indignation.

"I saw your white flag for help," Melva teased.

Immediately the two women began to discuss the upcoming celebration. Mrs. Dietz set out coffee, milk and a platter of bagels spread with cream cheese, and surprised Robyn by sitting down at the table with them. It was plain to see the housekeeper was relieved that re-inforcements had appeared, and Robyn began to look at Melva's arrival in a different light. She'd always liked the older woman, and Melva's talkative, outgoing personality was especially welcome in a tense situation.

Becky ignored the adults as she ate her bagel and

scribbled in a small notebook. A determined set to her little chin warned Robyn that she might turn out to be a real pain. Obviously, she was caught up in some kind of fantasy about being Nancy Drew.

"Have you seen the morning papers?" Melva asked, digging into her ample brocade bag. "There's a nice piece in the society column about Stoneview's upcoming birthday bash."

Lynette had informed Robyn in their last telephone conversation that she'd sent some information to the newspaper. Robyn silently groaned as she read the society item.

A centennial house celebration planned at the Stoneview estate. Lynette Valcourt, owner of the historical hundred-year-old house on Chataqua Lake, has invited all former occupants and their relatives to a birthday party. Invitations have been sent to members of the five families who have owned the property, asking them to bring their memories and stories to share at the celebration. Prominent residents who have had ties with Stoneview through the years will also be included in the guest list. Mrs. Valcourt hinted that a written history of the estate is likely to result from the celebration.

Robyn handed the newspaper back to Melva. "Well, that article should insure a bunch of publicity hounds and curious gawkers. Maybe we should just hang Open House signs on the doors?"

"It's going to be okay, honey." Melva reached over

and patted her hand. "Your grandmother is going to be proud of you."

Robyn bit back a caustic reply. If the least little thing went wrong, she knew what her grandmother's reaction would be—and it wouldn't be a show of pride.

"Who is that with Nick?" Melva asked as she looked out a window at two men walking toward the house from the cottage.

Robyn's cup clicked against the saucer as she nervously set it down. She hoped her voice sounded natural and relaxed. "Oh, that's Brian Keller. He's a relative of Joe Keller, the prizefighter. He arrived yesterday and Nick put him to work."

"Hmm, nice looking," Melva said in a slightly flirtatious tone that belied her age. "He carries himself well. I like a graceful masculine stride like that, don't you?"

Robyn wanted to deny she'd even noticed. She wasn't about to admit she'd spent a restless night thinking about the way they'd moved together on the dance floor. Remembering how deftly his firm body had brushed against hers with every spin still aroused an excitement she'd felt dancing with him.

"Oh, they're coming in," Melva said merrily.

Robyn braced herself. She was determined to keep a formal distance between herself and Brian Keller, mentally assuring herself that if he proved to be a problem, she'd ask him to leave. He had no right to impose on her hospitality and create an embarrassing situation for her.

A short hall led from the outside, past the breakfast

room, to the kitchen, and the two men might have walked by if Melva hadn't stopped them.

"Hey, Nicholas," she called out. "We've got a list a mile long for you."

Nick frowned until he saw who was yelling at him, then he gave Melva a wide grin. "Uh-oh, fasten down the hatches. Trouble just blew in."

"You better believe it." Melva sparked right back. "Come give this old lady a hug. I knew you when you were wet behind the ears."

"That's an exaggeration." Nick bent over the back of her chair, gave her a bear hug around the shoulders, and then studied her with exaggerated interest. "You haven't aged a day, my lovely."

BRIAN WATCHED the exchange with more than casual interest, and could have sworn the lady flushed. *Interesting,* he thought. He was wondering how to introduce himself when Robyn surprised him by speaking up.

"Melva, this is Brian Keller—"

"Oh, yes, you told me," Melva said. "A relative of the flamboyant Joe Keller." She held out her hand. "I'm Darrel Sheldon's mother. It's a real pleasure to meet you, Brian."

"Likewise," he said, smiling and adding silently, *More than you know.*

Finding out what had been going on in the Sheldon family when the tragedy happened was a top priority. In most crimes the place to start an investigation was with the people most involved. He was hoping this outgoing lady might prove to be a source of valuable information.

"This is my granddaughter," Melva said proudly.

Becky kept her eyes on her notebook, until Melva reached out and touched her hand. "Becky, say hello to Mr. Keller."

Rebecca Sheldon. Brian instantly registered the name of the kidnapped baby. Yes, she'd be eleven by now.

Without much interest, the little girl dutifully said, "Hello."

"I'm happy to meet you, Becky."

"Why?" she asked with childish honesty. "Is it 'cause you know I'm famous?"

The sincerity of the question stopped Brian for a moment. "Are you? Famous?"

Before the little girl could answer, Melva said firmly, "Not now, Becky. Not now."

The child slumped back in her chair, started chewing on her pencil and didn't say any more.

"I was telling Melva you'd arrived early and offered to help Nick," Robyn added hastily, as if embarrassed to have Brian know she'd already mentioned him.

"And I can sure use the help," Nick said, scowling. "It's going to be touch and go to get the boathouse ready. Robyn, I really think you should have an insurance adjustor come out and evaluate the damage. The door frames are bent, the wrought-iron staircase is loose, and I don't think we can salvage either one of the boats. Your grandmother will want to put in a claim for the damage. Do you know who handles her insurance?"

Robyn frowned. "I'm not sure."

"I bet it's either John Parker or his son, Todd." Melva spoke up, and then added for Brian's benefit, "John

Parker is the one who sold Stoneview to my son, Darrel, and his wife, Sybil." Then she smiled knowingly at Robyn. "Is Todd still sweet on you? I bet he'd love to have an excuse to come calling."

The way Robyn's cheeks suddenly colored, Brian silently wondered about Todd Parker. *An admirer? A boyfriend? Or even a lover?*

"I'll check," Robyn said, sidestepping Melva's remarks. "Meanwhile, don't stop work, Nick. I know my grandmother will want everything ready—even if she has to foot the bill for extra time."

"Good enough." Nick nodded his bushy head. "Let's get back to it, Brian."

"When you have a minute," Melva interjected quickly, "would one of you fine gentlemen bring in our things from the car so Becky and I can get settled?" She turned to Robyn. "What room shall we take?"

"Which one would you like? I'm afraid the cleaning maids won't be here for a couple of days. Things could be dusty and you'll have to get linens for the beds."

"No problem. How about the west guest room? I always loved the sunsets. Becky can have the smaller room next door."

"No." Becky stood up, her mouth set in a determined pout. "I have to stay in the nursery!"

"Now Becky…" Melba began.

"It says so right here!" She thrust out a junior detective manual, showing a boy and girl wearing Sherlock Holmes hats, holding flashlights and peering at something in a darkened room.

"Child, child." Melva gave an exasperated laugh.

"Why don't you play a different game? I mean, pretend you're a pirate, looking for treasure. You could draw a map and—"

"No, Grammie," she said firmly, as her little chin jutted at a pugnacious angle. "I want to find my own treasure. The one Daddy paid to get me back. I heard him tell Mama nobody knows what happened to it." Her eyes sparkled. "There's all kind of places in the house where I can look."

Brian mentally groaned. Hell, that's all he needed—some kid snooping around underfoot. Obviously, she wasn't going to be put off by anything her grandmother said. She was one determined girl.

"There isn't any nursery, Becky," Robyn said smoothly, obviously trying to put an end to the discussion. "That's my bedroom now."

"Goodie!" Becky clapped her hands. "I can stay in your room. We can look for clues together."

"Sorry, honey, but you'll have to stay in the room your grandmother chooses."

Becky pouted, sat back down with a thump, crossed her arms against her chest. Brian took advantage of the moment to volunteer to bring in the luggage. He had been hoping for a chance to survey the second floor. Whoever had taken the baby from the nursery had used either the main stairway or the servants' stairs. He wanted to see how easily that could be done with parents sleeping in the master bedroom on the same floor.

According to official reports, the nursemaid, Heather Fox, had not awakened when the baby was stolen, and denied that she'd had any contact with strangers before the kidnapping. When she was found strangled on the grounds, unanswered questions about the kidnapping had mounted.

As Melva rose to her feet, she motioned to Brian to accompany her. When they reached the five-car garage, she pointed out a new-model, bright red sports car. "That's mine. You should see the looks I get when I whiz by," she said, laughing. "Sometimes I wave or wink, and watched people's mouths drop open. It's a blast. I may be a sixty-five-year-old lady but I'm sure not going to act like one."

As Melva continued to chatter, Brian realized she might be a geyser of gossipy information that might prove very enlightening. He'd bet very little went on around her that she didn't notice.

"I had to bring party clothes along with everything else." She pointed to various sizes of matching suitcases in the trunk and back seat. "We're not like you men, who only need a dark suit to look great."

Brian nodded. The invitation had not specified formal attire, but he had already made arrangements to pick up a tailored suit in Chataqua the day before the party.

Melva took two small cosmetic cases, and Brian managed the larger suitcases. On the way upstairs to the west guest room, she chatted about this great idea of Lynette's to celebrate the house's one-hundred-year birthday.

"I guess all five families are going to be represented. It's too bad your uncle couldn't come. You'll have to send him pictures."

"I'll do that," Brian lied.

The six bedrooms on the second floor were placed with an adjoining bathroom between them—except for the master suite, which had its own spacious bath. The guest room that Melva had chosen was a corner one with windows looking out the north and west sides of the house.

Brian quickly set down the suitcases, and waved away her thanks. "I need to help Nick with the boathouse repairs."

"Will we see you at dinner?" Melva asked as she walked with him into the hall.

"I don't know. I'm bunking with Nick."

"Well, that doesn't mean he gets to monopolize you. I'll talk to Robyn and Mrs. Dietz. After all, you are a guest, first of all. You should eat with us."

Not really, Brian silently corrected her. Aloud he said, "Then I'll look forward to seeing you at dinner, Melva."

As he made his way slowly down the hall, he identified the front master suite, and wondered which of the remaining bedrooms might be the original nursery. When he heard Robyn's voice and Becky's high-pitched, childish response coming through an open door at the far end of the hall, he had his answer.

Apparently Becky was still carrying on her crusade to bunk with Robyn, and Brian could hear the exasperation in Robyn's voice. He decided to come to her rescue, and get a glimpse of the old nursery himself.

"Oh, there you are, Becky," he said, giving a light tap on the open door before he went in. "Your grandmother asked me to look for you. I brought up the suitcases and she's ready for you to unpack your things—in your room." He stressed the last words.

Robyn sent him a grateful smile, and with a firm hand on Becky's back, guided her to the door. "There are still swings and monkey bars under the trees at the side of the house. I bet you'd enjoy spending some time there."

The disgusted look Becky gave her clearly showed what she thought of that suggestion. Obviously, her role as a detective did not include such childish activities, but she seemed to know arguing wasn't going to work. The girl flounced out with a scowl that clearly indicated she wasn't through trying to get her way.

Robyn turned to Brian as they heard her footsteps fading down the hall. "Thanks, I needed rescuing," she admitted.

"She's something else, isn't she?" Brian agreed with a wry smile. "In a way, you have to admire the kid. I mean, she's enjoying her status as the kidnapped baby as a kind of celebrity, and not as a victim. Even as young as she is, she seems to be very purposeful."

"And what a purpose." Robyn sighed. "I hope this fixation isn't going to ruin the rest of her life. Sometimes I have the feeling that the tragedy is still waiting to be played out."

"What do you mean?"

"It's nothing I can really define." A pained look came into her eyes as she told him about finding Nick's cat wailing pitifully from the very spot where Heather Fox's strangled body had been found. "I know it's foolish, but sometimes I have a feeling this drama is somehow still with us."

"Trusting your feelings is pretty important some-times."

"Maybe." She sighed again. "It's easy to let one's imagination weave all kinds of nonsense. Becky shouldn't be trying to stir up something better left alone."

"Maybe if the truth came out—" Brian started to argue.

"And what good would that do?" Robyn demanded sharply. "What's over is over."

Her tone brooked no argument. He could imagine her fury when she found out how he had deceived her so he could stir up the past she wanted left alone.

As they'd been talking, he'd made a quick survey of her bedroom. The long room had probably been two small ones originally, and had been opened up to form a kind of alcove at one end, which he suspected had served as the nursery. Whoever had taken the baby would have had to pass through the single door at the nanny's end of the room, not once, but twice, coming and going.

"Nice view," he remarked, casually looking out one of the tall windows.

"Yes, I'm glad I'm on the lake side."

He pretended to admire the scene while his mind considered one of the windows as a possible entrance point to the room. Conceivably, a very tall ladder might access the narrow decorative ridge that trimmed the house, and one of the tall oak trees growing close to the wall might have allowed an agile kidnapper to gain entrance into the room that way.

In either case a logical question remained. Why

hadn't the nursemaid heard someone coming into the nursery through a window? Removing a screen and raising the glass surely would have created enough noise to waken her.

Maybe she hadn't been sleeping in her own bed that night? The possibility opened up some interesting avenues, and he mentally filed the question for future examination.

"Well, I'd better hunt up Nick and see what's next," he said, turning away from the windows.

He was surprised when she followed him out of the room and walked down the stairs with him. As they rounded the landing between the first and second floors, she pointed out two massive stained glass windows.

"My grandmother just had them restored. It took eight months to complete. They're lovely, aren't they?"

"Yes, lovely," he agreed, because they were. But it was muted light through the tinted glass, like the brush of rose petals touching her face, that brought a tightness in his chest. Her reddish brown hair glowed with strokes of fiery gold, and if she'd remained stationary in front of the windows, he might have questioned the reality of her living, breathing loveliness. Just looking at her, he felt his senses reel. Logically, he accepted the fact that being around Robyn Valcourt was a necessary part of the assignment, and he'd better not blow it. Unfortunately, a man's feelings, desires and longings were seldom logical.

When they reached the ground floor, Robyn turned toward the library. "I'd better call John Parker first. My grandmother doesn't make a move without his approval."

"He's a lawyer?" Brian asked innocently, knowing damn well exactly who he was. He'd been his father's attorney, and when the rest of the community had fostered suspicions about Dr. Donovan's relationship with Heather Fox, and the return of the kidnapped baby on his doorstep, John Parker had been one of the few who'd stood by Brian's father and debunked any suggestion that he was connected to either crime.

Robyn raised an eyebrow at his question. "Didn't you know that the Parkers bought Stoneview from your uncle? They lived here while their son, Todd, was growing up, and when Mrs. Parker died, they sold the property to the Sheldons."

Brian pretended ignorance. "Oh, I didn't know that."

"Mr. Parker will be here for the celebration."

"And Todd, too?"

"I expect that he and his father will be dropping by before then." Once again, he detected a slight rise in color in her cheeks. "Now, if you'll excuse me, I'd better make that call." She turned and disappeared into the library.

Brian left the house and headed toward the lake and boathouse. Things were moving faster than he'd planned. He wasn't concerned about meeting Todd Parker, who had been about twenty years old at the time of the kidnapping, and certainly wasn't running in the same circles with punk high school kids. Brian had no memory of him at all, but Todd's father was a different matter.

As a young boy, Brian had been in the company of his own dad and John Parker once or twice. After the notoriety of the Sheldon kidnapping, and his father had moved the family away, Brian couldn't remember seeing Mr. Parker again, but it might have happened. It was possible that the lawyer could have visited his father in Boston, and seen recent family pictures of Brian.

Would John Parker connect the dark-haired, adult Brian Keller with Buddy Donovan, the blond-headed, gangly adolescent son of his old doctor friend?

Chapter Four

When Robyn gave her name to John Parker's secretary, the woman put the call right through to his office.

"Robyn, dear, how are you?" The lawyer's greeting was warm and personal. "Are you all ready for the big day?"

"Don't I wish," Robyn answered frankly. "It's one of those times when I feel as if I'm taking two steps forward and four backward. Anyway, I'm calling about some damage that was done to the boathouse and a couple of the boats during a winter ice storm awhile back. I already have repairs under way, but I need to check on the insurance and file a claim."

"Well, Todd's company has the insurance, you know. It's worked out very nicely to have his agency in the same office building." He chuckled. "Kinda gives me a chance to keep an eye on my son. I'm still hoping Todd will settle down one day with a nice gal like you, and make me a grandpa."

Robyn's hand tightened on the receiver, but she managed to respond airily. "You'd make a great grandpa, John. About the boathouse, would you explain the situation to Todd? I'm really swamped and I have a dozen other calls to make."

"Of course. We're all glad to help," he answered readily. "You're special, you know that."

Robyn exchanged a few more pleasantries, thanked him and ended the conversation as quickly as was politely possible.

Last Christmas when she'd been home for the holidays, she and Todd Parker had been an item. At the time she'd been restless, and disgruntled about her lack of a personal life. Todd had come on the scene, a personable man-about-town, older than she, and for a few weeks she'd enjoyed a whirlwind holiday romance that stopped just short of any physical intimacy. When she returned to her college duties, she'd realized her feelings for Todd were not deep and lasting, and she'd quickly put an end to the romantic relationship. Todd had tried the usual routine of calls, flowers, and even made a couple of short visits to see her, but the momentary romantic flame had gone out. She hadn't seen Todd since she'd been back, and she'd hoped this insurance business wouldn't encourage his attentions again.

When she left the library a few minutes later, she found Melva in the butler's pantry, busily making a selective inventory for the dinner party. Numerous sets of dishes, glassware, silver and goblets were visible in cabinets that rose from the floor almost to the ceiling. Years of Lynette's entertaining as an ambassador's wife had resulted in a dinnerware collection that would be more than enough for the number of expected guests.

Robyn had no idea how much the collection was valued, but the silverware alone must be worth thousands of dollars.

"What fun this is!" Melva bubbled. "I decided we ought to choose a china pattern first, and then select glassware and table service that harmonize with it. What do you think?"

"I'll leave it up to you," Robyn said gratefully. "Mrs. Dietz knows where the linens are for the formal dining room. She has extra help coming to set the table. I know we'll need a couple more serving stations, but the main table can be extended to hold all the invited guests."

"It will be like old times." Melva had a faraway look in her eyes. "Darrel and Sybil gave some wonderful dinner parties. I really hated it when they sold this place. They just couldn't put the ugliness that happened behind them." She sighed. "It isn't as if bad spirits haunt the place."

Isn't it? Robyn questioned silently. She'd read plenty of ghost stories about a restless spirit remaining to haunt the living, unable to move on until a death had been avenged. Remembering Sinbad's mournful wailing, she felt the skin on her neck prickle. There were times when the murdered nursemaid's presence seemed very real.

"Where's Becky?" Robyn wished she had the girl's innocent acceptance of the past.

"She's supposed to be sitting out in the gazebo reading, or making notes or something. I hope she's not going to pester you…about the nursery and all. Once Becky gets something in her head, it sticks like glue."

"She's certainly bright and tenacious," Robyn agreed.

"Kinda makes you wonder about her natural parents, doesn't it?" Melva mused. "Not that Darrel and Sybil would trade her for the world. I've never seen adoptive parents so crazy about a kid." She laughed. "And me, too."

Mrs. Dietz poked her head in the pantry at that moment to ask how many there were going to be for dinner.

"Just three," Robyn answered. "Melva, Becky and me."

Melva interrupted her quickly. "Oh, my, I'm afraid I said something to Brian Keller about dinner. I just assumed he would join us—his being a guest and all. Isn't that all right?"

"It's all right with me," Mrs. Dietz assured her. "We're having pot roast. I can throw in a couple of extra potatoes and carrots."

"All right, then we'd better include Nick, too," Robyn decided quickly. "He's not much for socializing, and usually prefers to do his own thing, but we'd better ask."

LATER THAT AFTERNOON, as Brian was leaving the boathouse, he saw Robyn coming down the sidewalk with a man of average height, light-brown hair, wearing tailored slacks and an open-collared sports shirt. Brian suspected he might be Todd Parker, from the intimate way he was smiling at Robyn, and from the way that name had brought color to her cheeks when he'd been mentioned.

Brian was suddenly conscious of his own disheveled appearance. His khaki pant legs were wet to his knees from wading in the water, his cotton shirt soiled with mud splotches, and he was sure shocks of unruly hair hung on his forehead. He'd never looked worse. So what? He wasn't in competition for the lady's approval, and it was better if Todd Parker didn't have any interest in him at all.

When Robyn introduced them, Todd nodded but didn't offer to shake hands, and Brian wasn't even sure the Joe Keller connection registered. Todd seemed more interested in the condition of the boathouse than meeting another invited guest.

"Wow, what a mess," he exclaimed as he surveyed the damage from the outside. "You're right, Robyn. Lynette's going to have a fit if we don't get this cleaned up before the celebration."

Nick appeared in the side door of the boathouse, and when he saw Todd, he motioned to him.

"Come look at this," he called.

AS THE TWO MEN disappeared inside, Robyn turned away and slowly walked out on the nearby pier without looking at Brian. Let him join the other men. She needed some downtime. If she returned to the house, she'd likely be engulfed in the nonstop demands coming from every direction. At the moment she wasn't up to playing hostess to anyone—not even Brian Keller.

She eased down on the edge of the pier. A reflection of the blue sky and white clouds played upon the water, and she drew a relaxing deep breath as she gazed across the lake.

A moment later, when she heard a movement behind her, she knew that Brian had followed.

Without saying anything, he sat down beside her, letting his long legs dangle over the water as he leaned back on his arms.

She purposefully avoided looking at him. Earlier, when she'd told Todd about Brian's relationship to Joe Keller, and described his early arrival a week before the party, Todd had been immediately suspicious.

"It could be a setup," he'd warned her. "I wouldn't trust him for a minute, honey. Your grandmother's valuable objects in the house would tempt any thief."

"Oh, I'm sure his early arrival is innocent enough," she had argued, even though she knew Todd spoke the truth.

"Don't be naive. This guy's willingness to help could be a ruse," Todd had insisted. "More likely, he wants the chance to look around and see what's worth taking. Then when the time is right, he'll make his move."

"That's pretty melodramatic," Robyn had replied lightly. "You've been reading too many mysteries, Todd."

"I wouldn't trust anyone with a drop of Keller blood in him. Plenty of wild stories have floated around about what went on in this place back then." He shook his head. "I don't like it, honey. I don't like it at all."

Neither did Robyn, but she wasn't sure exactly why. She couldn't really believe Brian Keller was some kind of con man. She'd readily admit his presence was disturbing in some way, but only on a deeper, more personal level.

She was very aware of his disturbing company as he sat beside her on the pier, and it had nothing to do with a concern over her grandmother's silverware.

She was surprised when Brian continued to act as if

she wasn't even there. She began to relax as a soothing silence enveloped them. The only sound was the ebb and flow of waves on the shoreline caused by a scattering of sailboats flitting lightly over the water like colorful butterflies.

The tension in Robyn's neck began to ease, and when she finally turned to look at him, she half expected him to destroy the peaceful moment with a reminder that there was no time for this kind of wasteful idleness. Instead, he was peering down into the water, smiling broadly as if something amused him.

"What is it?" she asked, puzzled, trying to follow his gaze.

"Didn't you see that saucy bass swishing around, just asking to meet up with a frying pan?"

She looked and caught only a glimpse of a silver tail. "So you're a fisherman?"

"Used to be. How about you?"

"I like seafood," she admitted, "but only served on a platter with tasty sauce."

"Too bad. Fishing is a very relaxing pastime."

"Well, that lets me out," she answered wryly.

"What? Fishing or relaxing?"

"Both, I'm afraid."

"That's too bad. You ought to try fishing sometime. Maybe we could scare up a pole or two, tomorrow or the next day, and you could give it a try?"

She looked at him as if he'd suddenly started talking gibberish. The suggestion was too ridiculous for a response. "I better get back to the house before Melva and Mrs. Dietz send someone after me."

"You should try playing hooky sometime," he chided as they both got to their feet. "You might like it."

She laughed. "I just might at that."

As they walked away from the pier, heading for the house, neither Nick nor Todd were in sight. Brian wondered what effect Todd Parker's presence was going to have on his freedom to move about the estate.

"Nick said he expected to be hiring more help now that the insurance company is involved," Brian commented as casually as he could.

"Yes, there'll be a crew out tomorrow to take over," Robyn replied, and added smoothly, "There's no need to impose on you any longer. I'm sure you can find more entertaining things to do before the celebration than spending your time here."

Brian recognized a red alert in her words and attitude. His welcome was crumbling. A few hours ago she had been grateful for his extra help. Now, she was inviting him to leave. What had changed her? The arrival of Todd Parker on the scene?

"Maybe I shouldn't hang around," he admitted, gambling on a sudden spurt of intuition as he added, "I wouldn't want to intrude on any love nest, that's for sure. If you and Todd Parker—"

"No, it's not that," Robyn interrupted. "We're just friends."

"Sorry!" Brian instantly apologized. "I didn't mean to hit a sensitive chord. Just couldn't help picking up on the way he was relating to you. Kinda possessive."

"You're very perceptive." Her lips tightened. "That's

exactly the way he treats me." She was obviously a little embarrassed that she'd revealed this personal insight to him.

Brian nodded in a sympathetic way. "Some men are like that, I guess."

"I didn't mean to suggest that your presence is unwelcome, Brian," she told him, as if the thought had just crossed her mind that having a third party around might deflect some unwanted attention from Todd.

Brian could almost see the wheels turning in her head as she quickly changed tactics about his leaving. "I'm sure there will be plenty of times when an extra pair of hands will be invaluable. You're certainly welcome to stay."

"I'd like to help out where I can," he assured her. "I need to take a run across the lake in the morning and pick up some things in Chataqua. How about my doing some errands for you?"

She hesitated, as if weighing the idea.

"Or better still, why don't you come along?" he added impulsively.

"Oh, I couldn't," she said quickly, shaking her head.

"Why not? I bet you could use a change of scenery for a couple of hours."

"Yes, I could, but I have a cleaning crew coming tomorrow that needs supervision."

"And Melva and Mrs. Dietz couldn't handle them?"

"Of course they could, but…"

He could tell she was wavering. A glint of wistfulness softened the misty blue of her eyes as she said, "I'll think about it and check with you in the morning."

He was afraid to push too hard, but there was something pensive in her manner that hinted she was seriously considering accepting his invitation.

"Melva said you were having dinner with us tonight," she stated as she paused on the front steps of the house.

"She invited me. Is that all right?"

"Of course. Sevenish?" She added, "Ask Nick to come, too."

After she'd disappeared into the house, Brian headed for the cottage. He'd been tense there for a few minutes when she had invited him to leave. He wasn't sure exactly what she was thinking, and what was threatening to jeopardize his presence in the house, but he was relieved that he'd navigated some dangerous rapids.

He thought about the few harmonious moments sitting on the pier, when they'd related to each other outside the boundaries of the present situation. Then he'd been foolish enough to suggest they spend time together fishing, and he'd felt her instant withdrawal. It didn't take a genius to know that getting cozy with Robyn Valcourt wasn't in his best interests any way he looked at it. Unless he could use her as a viable key in his investigation, he'd better leave well enough alone.

As Brian bathed and dressed for dinner in presentable gray slacks and a black-and-white sports shirt, his thoughts settled on Melva Sheldon. At the moment, the gossipy lady seemed to be his best source of information. Living in the house with her son and daughter-in-law at the time of the kidnapping and murder, she might still retain some important information about what had happened before, during and after.

One of the things that puzzled Brian the most was the lack of a motive for killing Heather Fox after the baby had been returned. The police had advanced the theory that she knew who the kidnapper was, and had been killed to insure her silence. If that was the case, why hadn't she been murdered the night of the kidnapping instead of a day after the ransom had been paid?

The timing *was* off. That gut feeling told him there was something more to her death. But what?

When Brian told Nick they'd been invited to dinner at the big house, he shook his head. "Thanks, but no thanks. I enjoy eating too much to suffer a bunch of idle talk about stuff I don't care a fig about. No, siree, it's my night to spend a couple of hours at Al's Pub and Grill. Good food, cold beer on tap and lots of good old boys to keep me company." He slapped Brian on the back. "You're welcome to come along."

"Thanks, maybe some other time." Brian wasn't about to turn down a dinner invitation that might strengthen his position at Stoneview.

"I guess we don't have to bust our backs on the boat-house anymore," Nick told him. "The insurance company is going to put some contracted repairmen on the job. I think Todd Parker is afraid he'll be put on the rack if the job isn't finished by the time Mrs. Valcourt gets back." Nick gave Brian a weary grin. "Better him than us."

"Is Todd Parker a personal friend of the Valcourts?" Brian asked innocently.

"I don't know about the old lady, but he's been hanging around Robyn like they might have something going."

"Is it serious?"

Nick shrugged. "Who knows? They were hitting it off pretty good last Christmas, always coming or going to some party or another."

"He's not in law practice with his father?" Brian asked, as if he didn't know the answer.

"Rumor is Todd couldn't cut the mustard when it came to law school, and his father settled him in the insurance business instead. I think Robyn could do better. Between you and me, there'd be a dozen fellows hanging around her if her grandmother didn't monopolize all her time."

Brian started to ask about the father, John Parker, but Nick was through chatting. Brian was afraid if he pushed too hard for information, Nick would resent it and clam up altogether.

"I'll probably beat you home," Nick said as he turned away and started up the stairs to clean up. "I'm too darn tired to do much tonight."

Brian waited until Nick had driven away in his pickup before leaving the cottage. He wondered if Robyn would be sociable during dinner, or maintain her distant lady-of-the-house manner.

Melva greeted him as he entered the mansion, and he learned it was neither. "Robyn wanted me to apologize. She feels she wouldn't be good company tonight, and has decided to have a tray in her room. Where's Nick?"

"He sends his regrets, too," Brian answered.

"Oh, my, Becky ate earlier with Mrs. Dietz and now she's upstairs reading a book. So I'm afraid it's…" She faltered.

"Just you and me," Brian finished gallantly, quickly assessing the situation. Even though his manly pride smarted because Robyn had passed up having dinner with him, he welcomed this chance to guide Melva's ever-flowing chatter into areas that might be of value.

As they settled themselves in the cozy small dining room, Mrs. Dietz served them, muttering as she set down steaming dishes in front of them. Obviously, she wasn't happy about preparing dinner for five and having only two show up.

"Mrs. Dietz is a wonderful cook," Melva said, loudly enough for her to hear as she left the room. In a softer, confidential tone, she added, "It never hurts to butter up the help. I keep telling that to my daughter-in-law, but Sybil is just too much of a perfectionist." Melva sighed. "I guess it's because life has disappointed her."

"In what way?" Brian asked casually as he picked up a decanter sitting on the table and filled Melva's wine-glass.

"Children," Melva answered in a regretful tone. "She and Darrel spent a lot of years and a pile of money trying to have a family. It was hard on Sybil. She knew how much Darrel wanted kids." Melva lowered her voice. "I thought their marriage was in real trouble. Being the mother-in-law, I tried to keep out of it, but I could see what a great father my son would be. Sybil was dead set against adoption, but when Darrel started checking into it, I think she finally realized she'd better give in."

"Sometimes adoption is the best way," Brian agreed. "And Becky is a charmer if I ever saw one."

"Isn't she?" Melva laughed. "Smart as a whip. When that tiny baby girl came into their lives, both Darrel and Sybil were ecstatic. I couldn't ask for a more delightful granddaughter. She really keeps us on our toes."

Brian nodded, chuckling.

"Darrel has wanted to adopt more children, but I think Sybil is afraid the next one wouldn't turn out as good. She's kind of a negative person, you know. I think it's because she was caught in that corporate rat race. She's very possessive of Darrel and Becky." Melva pursed her lips. "We've had a few set-tos now and again."

Brian wasn't surprised. "You've lived with them a long time?"

"Before they got Becky. And after what happened, I was glad I was there. Sybil and Darrel needed help getting over the horrible scare. It's been a good arrangement, I think. Becky's enough of a handful for all three of us."

"The kidnapping must have been hard on all of you."

Melva took a generous sip of her wine. "It was, and when we got the baby back, we all thought the nightmare was over."

Brian nodded sympathetically. "The nursemaid's murder must have been a shock."

"None of us could believe it. Heather was such a wonderful nanny. The family doctor, Dr. Donovan, recommended her."

Brian was a little startled to hear his father's name mentioned so casually. "How old was the nanny?" he asked, even though he knew the answer.

"Late twenties, I think. Nice looking, but not the least bit stylish. She didn't show much refinement, if you know what I mean. I think she'd had a rough up-bringing, even though she never talked about it. She wasn't afraid to stand her ground, though."

"What makes you say that?"

Melva took a bite of chicken before she answered. "Well, when Heather first came, Sybil had her wearing white uniforms, but that soon changed. Very quietly and stubbornly, Heather began wearing simple skirts and different colored blouses, and because the young woman was so good and competent with the baby, Sybil decided not to make an issue of the uniforms." Melva gave a soft laugh. "A couple of times I coaxed Heather into letting me fix her hair all fancy-like. I teased her about how she should get herself a fellow and have a little fun."

"Did she go out much?" Brian asked, intent upon finding out as much about the victim as he could. There were too many details missing and too many unanswered questions about Heather Fox's personal life.

Melva looked thoughtful. "I kinda suspected there might be a fellow in the picture, but the police didn't come up with anyone."

"What did she do on her days off?"

"Mostly nothing. I mean, she stayed pretty much to herself."

"How about visitors?

Melva shook her head. "Not even a member of her family, poor thing. Ah well, what is past is past."

Brian could tell from the way she shrugged that she

was ready for a change of subject. "What about you, Brian? I don't see any sign of a wedding band. How have you escaped the matrimonial snare?"

"Just lucky, I guess," he quipped, and poured her more wine. "Some of us guys were just born to be bachelors."

Melva rose to the challenge. For the rest of the meal she bombarded him with all the reasons why every man needed a good woman to complete his life.

Deftly Brian deflected her personal questions, and made several attempts to turn the conversation in productive veins, but failed. Melva was through talking about family. Making excuses for turning in early, he didn't linger over coffee and dessert.

When he returned to the cottage, he decided to take advantage of Nick's absence to search the premises. A complete picture of even the most innocent bystander might help him build a scenario for the two crimes. Nick had been no more than thirty at the time, and maybe he'd been closer to what had happened than it appeared.

Sinbad greeted Brian with a begging "meow" and earned a pat on his sleek head as Brian headed up the stairs, and down the hall to Nick's bedroom. As he opened the door, the cat followed at his heels and jumped up on the unmade bed to watch.

One thing was sure, Brian thought as he looked around at the disheveled room, Nick would never know if something had been moved.

Several fishing poles leaned against the wall in one corner, next to a dusty guitar displaying three broken strings. A chest of drawers was piled high with a variety of storage boxes. The whole room seemed to verify that Nick was exactly what he appeared to be—a man with simple tastes.

Brian glanced at his watch. He didn't have much time if Nick meant what he'd said about just having a bite to eat and a couple of beers.

Where to start? A gateleg table seemed to serve as a kind of writing desk as well as a catch-all for mail and papers. After Brian deftly combed through bills, junk mail and newspaper flyers, he carefully replaced them in the same haphazard stacks. No personal correspondence was visible.

A noisy alarm clock sitting on a loaded bedside stand warned him that he'd already used up precious time. He turned his attention to the rest of the room, checking drawers and shelves for memorabilia of any kind.

Nothing.

Every time Brian heard the sound of a car on the nearby access road, he stiffened. Raising Nick's suspicions that he wasn't what he seemed to be would bring a halt to their friendly relationship. He quickened his search.

When a narrow closet door resisted his efforts to open it, Brian jerked on it with such force that the vibrations dislodged a high shelf just inside. He couldn't believe the pile of stuff that tumbled down. None of it was worth the time it took him to replace the shelf and all the things on it. Would Nick notice they'd been moved? Brian went quickly through the pockets of all the clothes hanging on the rack, but only found some sticks of chewing gum and a few coins.

He hurriedly gave his attention to a tall bureau and the various boxes piled on top. They were filled with screws, nails, washers and even some small tools.

Disappointed, Brian was about to put one of the wooden cigar boxes back on the dresser when the cat drew his attention to the bed.

Sinbad had found a half-eaten sandwich on a wobbly nightstand and was preparing to deposit it in the middle of Nick's bed.

"No!" A mess like that would be a telltale sign that someone had opened the bedroom door and let Sinbad inside.

As Brian lunged at the cat he lost his grip on the box he'd been holding. The cigar box hit the floor, the lid came off, and nails, bolts and screws bounced across the room.

In the ruckus, Sinbad scurried out with his prize.

Swearing, Brian scooped up some of the spilled contents, and was just putting them back when his fingers touched something on the bottom of the box. He turned it over.

"I'll be—!"

Mounted there was a small snapshot of a fair-haired young woman sitting on the lawn, smiling at the camera.

It was signed, "To sweet Nickolas with love, Heather."

Chapter Five

Carefully, Brian set the box back on top of the dresser and scurried around, picking up as many of the scattered metal objects as he could see. He knew some had rolled under the bed and other pieces of furniture, but he doubted Nick's casual housekeeping would bring them to light anytime soon.

As Brian replaced the lid on the box, he noticed that without all the contents it wasn't as heavy as before. If Nick picked up the wooden box from time to time so he could view the picture, undoubtedly he'd be aware of the change in weight almost immediately.

Brian quickly transferred a couple of small tools from one of the other dusty boxes and left everything piled up in the same haphazard way he'd found it.

He hesitated as he looked around the room at more clutter, but decided not to disturb anything else for the moment. He'd already gained an important insight and needed some time to put it in perspective.

When he went downstairs, he was relieved that Nick was not back yet. Apparently his good intentions to come back early had been waylaid. Casually, Brian wandered around the first floor rooms, trying to get a feel of the man who on the surface seemed to be steady and hardworking, with little ambition to make his life any different. But what about the deeper aspects of Nick's character? The hidden snapshot was proof that he had lied about not having any personal contact with Heather Fox.

Nothing in the investigative police reports Brian had looked at connected Nick in any way with the murdered nursemaid. If anyone had been aware of a relationship between them, it had not come to light. Maybe the police hadn't asked the right people.

Brian immediately thought of Melva Sheldon. The woman's friendliness and her willingness to gossip might bring to light some valuable information she didn't even know she had. The next time he had a chance to talk with her, he would try to steer the conversation in this direction. The mother-in-law obviously had been privy to a lot of things that went on at Stoneview when the Sheldons had lived there.

Back in his room, Brian stretched out on the bed and stared at the ceiling. He thought about Robyn Valcourt. He didn't doubt for a minute that if she had any suspicions he was up to some deceptive intent, she'd show him the door and slam it behind him.

Remembering her appealing combination of soft femininity and unwavering fortitude, he engaged in a fantasy that would have had the proper Miss Valcourt blushing to the roots of her fiery brown hair.

IT WAS MIDNIGHT BEFORE Robyn turned out the bedside lamp, still wide-awake and uptight. She'd avoided going down to dinner because she'd needed some private time to catch up on her thoughts and feelings. In those few minutes on the dock with Brian Keller, he had slipped past her emotional guard, and they'd shared a closeness that went beyond the kind of quiet communion she'd experienced with anyone.

Early in life, she'd felt an emptiness that no one had ever come close to filling. Putting up high barriers had been a way of protecting herself as she moved all over the globe with her parents, attending one embassy school after another. She'd always been the "foreigner," isolated and confined by protocol. She'd never became a part of the various cultures surrounding her, and her mother and father were too busy and involved for much parenting. Growing up, she learned to depend upon herself to fulfill her own emotional needs.

Robyn knew she was attractive to men, both in looks and money. A few of them, like Todd, had managed to keep her entertained for a brief period, but it never lasted, nor was any relationship deep enough to provide the sense of belonging that had been missing all her life. She'd come to terms with herself and her independent lifestyle, and was content with it. Wasn't she? How could she let a questionable relative of notorious Joe Keller get her off center? She already felt responsible for allowing this perfect stranger to have free rein on the premises, but the truth was she enjoyed his company. A quiet, sensible inner voice chided her. *Why not deal with it?* Certainly trying to avoid him the next few days wasn't practical. Why not accept his invitation to go with him to Chataqua? No doubt more familiarity would quickly put an end to any lingering attraction.

Satisfied with her decision, she gave her pillow a vigorous fluffing, and settled herself comfortably in bed for the night.

THE NEXT MORNING, Robyn woke up refreshed and ready for another busy day. Her high mood should have been a warning. She couldn't remember the last time she'd found herself humming as she showered and dressed.

After an early breakfast, she decided to walk over to the cottage and tell Brian her decision to accept his offer to take her across the lake to shop. She rationalized that at the same time, she could give Nick instructions for the day.

The two men were having breakfast when she knocked on the kitchen door. Peering through the half window, she saw Nick's heavy-lidded eyes grow round when he realized who it was. When he opened the door, she noted that he was unshaved and his bushy, uncombed hair stuck out at all angles.

"Good morning." She greeted him pleasantly as he seemed to be hesitating between asking her in and closing the door in her face. Then, as if realizing it was too late to mend his appearance, he muttered, "Morning."

"I needed to talk with you and Brian before the day gets started. May I come in?"

"Oh, yes…sorry." He quickly moved back.

Brian was standing at the stove, putting the finishing touches on an omelette. "Good morning." He greeted Robyn with a smile. "You're just in time for a one-of-a-kind, prize-winning omelette."

"Thanks, but I've had breakfast." Then she added quickly, "The coffee smells good, though. Mrs. Dietz is a tea drinker, so I usually have a cup of instant."

Brian quickly pulled out a chair for her. "One mug of hot java coming up."

Nick was obviously too ill-at-ease to sit down at the table again. He made a pretense of feeding Sinbad. Then he stroked his unshaved chin, mumbled an apology and excused himself.

Robyn raised a questioning eyebrow as Brian sat down opposite her and began eating his omelette.

"Isn't Nick feeling well?" she asked in an innocent tone, as if she didn't recognize a hangover when she saw one.

Brian avoided answering her question. "What's on the schedule for today?"

She took a sip of coffee before replying. "I do need to check on some things in Chataqua. Maybe we could take a quick run over there this morning…if your offer still holds?"

"Absolutely. It's a lovely day to take a spin on the lake," he added, with obvious pleasure that she'd decided to accept his invitation.

She stiffened slightly. His tone rang a warning bell. More than ever, she wanted to make sure the excursion didn't send the wrong message. The purpose of accepting his company was to try to quell the nebulous attraction he held for her.

"Will you tell Nick he needs to arrange for the damaged boats to be hauled away? I'll collect my things and meet you at the dock in thirty minutes." Her tone was that of a supervisor setting the agenda for the day.

After she'd left, Brian was puzzled by why she'd decided to accept his invitation. Her manner was rather guarded, as if she wasn't really looking forward to the boat ride. There was more than one car sitting in the garage. She could have driven into town on her own.

Nick grunted when Brian relayed Robyn's message to him, and when he told him about taking her to Chataqua that morning, he snapped, "Watch your step, boy. These rich gals can turn you inside out."

"Sounds like you're speaking from experience?"

Nick didn't take the bait, even though his remark about rich gals had all the earmarks of experience. Could Nick have been referring to Robyn? He might be harboring some unreal expectations and feelings for her. Nick certainly had been sour as he'd watched them dancing in the rec room.

And what about Heather Fox? The hidden photo was evidence that Nick and the murdered nursemaid had been closer than he was willing to admit to anyone.

Brian had heard Nick stumble up the stairs way after midnight, and his red-rimmed eyes and slack jaw the next morning verified Nick had made a night of it.

"An old drinking buddy of mine showed up," Nick confessed. "At the time, it seemed important that I match him drink for drink. Now I remember why I usually settle for a couple of beers."

BRIAN WAS WAITING at the pier when Robyn hurried down the sidewalk toward the boat. She looked terrific in a summery white dress with a colorful scarf looped over her shoulders. A short skirt revealed her shapely tanned legs as he offered her a guiding hand into the boat.

Instead of taking a seat in the bow, she stood beside him as he maneuvered the craft out into the lake. He wondered what she was thinking as a soft smile tugged at her lips and she lifted her face to the breeze.

"Would you like to steer?" he invited.

"No, thanks," she replied quickly.

It was too early for much traffic on the large lake, and they had it almost to themselves. Impulsively, he opened the throttle wide.

As the boat suddenly charged across the water, she was thrown slightly against him, and he braced her with his free arm. Not knowing what her reaction was going to be as she righted herself, he was relieved when she laughed and planted her feet more firmly on the deck.

"Ride 'em, cowboy," he teased.

Even though it had been years since he'd been in a speeding boat on this lake, a boyish exuberance came back, and Robyn seemed to be caught up in the same exhilaration. She remained in the circle of his arm, tossing her head back and lifting her face to the soft spray.

Brian deliberately made a zigzagging pattern in the water, and the boat leaned from side to side in a breathtaking ride. They seemed to have the bright morning all to themselves. Clutching each other, they maintained their balance, and even after Brian slowed the motor, they continued to lean together.

When Robyn raised her smiling face to his, he couldn't resist the soft moist shine of her pink lips. Impulsively he bent his head and lightly touched them with a kiss. The contact was fleeting, and her eyes widened with obvious surprise, but she didn't pull away from the circle of his arm.

He was tempted to prolong the crossing by making a wide swath in the lake before heading for one of the docks on the Chataqua side, but resisted the idea. As a rule he prided himself on being able to read a companion's moods and thoughts, but he'd never been around someone who challenged him the way Robyn Valcourt did. The more time he spent with her, the less confident he felt about being able to steer clear of a romantic catastrophe. Even now, his heartbeat quickened just looking at her. She seemed totally relaxed and happy, and her mood invited an intimacy that he couldn't afford. Too much depended on his continued presence at Stoneview, and he realized he could have blown everything with that one impulsive kiss.

As THEY WALKED a short block to Main Street, Robyn was intensely conscious of Brian's easy, smooth stride beside her, and the casual brushing of his thigh against hers. Her hair was windblown and her face was probably shiny from the water spray, but she didn't care.

Earlier, when the boat had skimmed across the water, leaving a foamy white wake behind it, she'd experienced an exhilarating sense of freedom. Her lips still tingled with the memory of his light, gentle kiss. By the time they'd docked, she'd put aside her intention to use the outing as a way of revising her feelings about Brian Keller, and mentally shoved all of Todd's suspicions and warnings away.

When they met a couple of her grandmother's friends coming toward them on the sidewalk, the older women's eyes fastened on Brian with open curiosity. Robyn just gave them a friendly nod and kept walking. She wasn't about to fill the gossip troughs by introducing him. She was glad he just smiled at the ladies as they passed, as if perfectly aware of her aversion to having to explain his company. Let them think what they would. The exciting ride and brief kiss had created a rare mood she didn't want anyone spoiling.

"I'll be a couple of hours, Brian," she said as they reached a main intersection. "Shall we meet at, say, eleven o'clock?"

"Sounds good. I need to check on a new suit I bought earlier, which needed a little altering. I'll pick up a few other things while I'm at it. How about we meet back at the pier where we left the boat?"

She nodded. Taking a list out of her leather bag, she said, "I guess I'll start by checking on the flower arrangements. Grandmother wants some rather complicated centerpieces." She gave him a quick smile as she headed across the street. She fought the impulse to look back and wave at him when she reached the other side.

As she tackled all the errands and solved a dozen unexpected problems, her exuberance stayed with her. When she checked the last errand off the list, and looked at her watch, she realized she was already nearly an hour late meeting Brian.

She didn't want him to think that she'd deliberately kept him waiting. As she hurried down the street, she passed a store window filled with sportsman's equipment. Her eyes fell on a display of fishing gear. A colorful poster showed a smiling couple standing proudly beside a string of fish. In her expansive mood, she remembered Brian's offer to take her fishing.

She'd bet there were fishing poles in the attic. There had been some stored in the boathouse before her grandmother had remodeled it. Maybe, just maybe, Robyn would take a look and see. Being with Brian Keller was liberating in a way she couldn't quite define, but one thing she was sure about. Having an exciting, stimulating man in her life was long overdue.

She arrived at the dock a little out of breath, and when she saw Brian sitting on one of the benches by the water, she mentally rehearsed an apology for being late. As she came up behind him, she realized he was talking on his cell phone. His end of the conversation swept over her like an icy shower.

"What would I ever do without you, Ginger?" he said in an affectionate tone. "I'll be in touch as often as I can, but there's no cell phone service on the other side of the lake. And the cottage phone is just an extension, so don't call me at the house. You'll never know how much I—"

Robyn didn't wait to hear more. She backed up and walked a short distance away. *Brian Keller had a woman in his life.* He was just entertaining himself with her company while he was around. She knew how that game worked….

She waited until he had finished talking, and then pretended she had just arrived. "I'm sorry I'm late," she apologized briskly.

"No problem," he assured her as he quickly rose to his feet and slipped his cell phone into the carrier on his belt. "Shall we try one of the lakeside restaurants for lunch?" he asked.

A cold appraisal in her eyes telegraphed her refusal even before she answered crisply, "I think not."

THE TRIP BACK ACROSS the lake was a sharp contrast to the companionable outing they'd had before. Brian couldn't imagine what had happened to send her back into that protective shell of hers. She sat on a seat behind him, silent and stiff. Had she had a run-in with someone about preparations for the party? Maybe he should have gone with her. He might have been able to handle some of the pressure for her.

After he'd picked up his suit and completed his shopping in quick order, he'd returned to the dock to make some telephone calls. Before leaving Augusta, he had engaged a female private investigator, Ginger Stephens, to secure as much background material on Heather Fox as possible. Ginger was about his age, smart, attractive and dependable, and he'd used her before on several cases. He had dialed her number while sitting on the bench, waiting for Robyn.

"I'm afraid I don't have much," she'd reported. "Heather Fox was raised on a farm in Iowa and ran away from home when she was sixteen. Her whereabouts remain unknown for the next five years until she surfaced at a practical nurse's training program in upper Maine. The school's records show that, after graduating, Heather was hired by several elderly people—and then she disappeared again. There's a two-year gap before she showed up at Chataqua and was hired by the Sheldons. I'm working on that."

"What about family?"

"None. Her parents died just about the time she enrolled in nurse's training. No siblings and no extended family could be found when she was murdered. I'm going to visit the nursing school and see if I can get a lead on any friends she might have made there."

They'd talked a few more minutes, and Brian promised to keep in touch. After he'd hung up, Robyn had arrived, displaying a one-hundred-and-eighty-degree turnaround in mood.

He couldn't figure her out. And what was worse, he was completely baffled by his own feelings about her. No other woman had been able to send his desires on such a roller coaster ride.

Given the circumstances, he was at a loss about how to maintain any balance at all in their relationship. And what puzzled him even more was why she had been able to touch him in a way other women he'd dated had failed to do.

With her sitting behind him, there was no way to initiate any conversation. Maybe, when they docked, he'd have a chance to find out what had happened in Chataqua to put her in such a mood.

But when they landed at Stoneview, she just gave him a curt nod, and headed up the sidewalk toward the house while he tended to securing the lines. From her dismissive manner, he suspected Stoneview's welcome mat would be pulled out from under him momentarily.

No one was in the boathouse, but as he passed a nearby gazebo, he heard a girlish giggle. Peering inside, he saw Becky sitting cross-legged on the wooden floor of the vine-covered arbor.

"Hi, Brian!" She motioned for him to join her.

He could see she'd been making sketches in a notebook. Stuff from her detective kit was spread all over the floor. Maybe her dedicated snooping might accidentally turn up something of interest. Spending a little time with her might be to his advantage.

"What's up?" he asked as he eased down on the floor beside her.

"I'm going to find a secret hiding place." Her eyes sparkled.

"Really?"

She nodded and showed him several childish drawings marking possible hidden rooms and passages in the house. "Just like in the movies."

"And what do you think is hidden there, Becky?"

She answered in a hushed whisper. "Secrets."

"What kind?" he asked in the same conspirator's tone.

"My daddy says there are all kinds of secrets in the house."

"What do you think he means by that?" Brian asked, not above quizzing an eleven-year-old girl, especially one as bright as Becky.

"I won't know till I find the secret place," she answered, in a tone that showed she thought the question was a dumb one. "Do you want to help me?"

He nodded solemnly. Playing Becky's game might serve as a cover for his own presence in questionable parts of the house if the occasion arose.

"You can be my deputy. And you have to wear this," she said with authority, handing him a plastic police badge.

He pinned it to his T-shirt and gave her a snappy salute. "Where shall we look first, Chief?"

Becky scrunched up her face as if thinking hard, but before she could answer, they heard Mrs. Dietz calling her.

"Becky! Becky! Answer me. Where are you, child?"

When Becky didn't move, Brian prodded, "Aren't you going to answer?"

"Oh, I suppose I have to," she grumbled. Scrambling to her feet and sticking her head out of the gazebo, she yelled back, "What do you want?"

"Your parents are here. You'd better come to the house right now."

The little girl's face crumpled. "Why'd they come so soon?"

"Maybe to take you home," Brian said as he helped her gather her things.

"I'm not going. I have to find the treasure first. Don't you see? Someone might try to kidnap me again."

Chapter Six

After Robyn left Nick securing the motorboat, she'd hurried into the mansion, struggling to regain her sense of equilibrium. It wasn't as if she'd never let herself be vulnerable, she acknowledged. There had been a few times when she'd opened up to a possible romantic relationship. Too soon she'd learned she was just another conquest, usually by someone courting the benefits of the Valcourt money and prestige. She was fortunate to have discovered Brian already had a woman in his life before she made a total fool of herself. *But I like him.* The admission was rather startling. Somehow Brian had managed to break the rigid patterns that had been ingrained in her from childhood. He'd been able to release hidden pockets of emotions she didn't even know still bubbled deep within her.

Having carefree fun had never been a part of her life. Even now she smiled, remembering the wild boat ride—and the unexpected kiss. She sighed. Whoever Ginger was, she was a damn lucky lady. Straightening her shoulders, Robyn vowed to mark the morning's experience a lesson learned.

A half-dozen cleaning ladies dressed in brown jumpsuits were all over the house. Mrs. Dietz was in a tizzy because Melva was issuing orders as if she were in charge.

"Ach! I'm the housekeeper here!" The German woman's accent always got heavy when she was upset. Olga Dietz wasn't a large woman, but intimidating when she braced her shoulders and dared anyone to disagree with her.

"Of course you are, Mrs. Dietz."

"Then you tell that woman I give the orders."

Robyn placated the housekeeper as best she could and went to find Melva. She wasn't in any of the first floor rooms, and before Robyn could check upstairs, the doorbell rang.

When she opened the door, Darrel and Sybil Sheldon stood on the front porch, smiling broadly at her.

"Hi, there, Robyn," Darrel greeted her. "We got back a couple of days early from our trip—"

"And thought we'd check and see how things are going," Sybil finished for him. Younger than her husband, she wasn't particularly physically attractive. She'd been struggling to make her way in corporate America when she married Darrel and gave up a career to be a wife and mother. Stylish blond hair framed a rather plain face, but she'd learned to make the best of what she had—with the help of expensive cosmetics and hairdressers. Sybil had always stayed pretty much to herself, even before they adopted Becky, and had since resisted Lynette's efforts to draw her into Chataqua's social whirl.

"How's that daughter of ours doing?" Darrel asked as they came into the house. He was the outgoing one in the couple, obviously taking after his mother. A successful businessman, he owned several franchises in different companies. In appearance, he was shorter than his wife by a couple of inches, and continually fought a middle-aged spread that expensive tailored clothes couldn't hide. Thinning dark hair framed a rather pudgy round face, but his people-pleasing personality made up for his less than handsome appearance. He was addicted to pipe smoking, and Stoneview had reeked of tobacco when he'd sold the house to the Valcourts. Lynette had made it clear Darrel wasn't to indulge in that "filthy" habit when she was around.

"Becky's just fine," Robyn answered readily, mentally keeping her fingers crossed. With everything else going on, she hadn't paid that much attention to the little girl. She trusted Melva was keeping a close eye on her.

"Driving you crazy, I'll bet," her father added proudly. "She's a pistol, isn't she?"

"Where is she?" Sybil asked, as if she wasn't satisfied with Robyn's vague answer.

"I'm not sure," Robyn had to admit. "I just this minute got back from Chataqua. We have a cleaning crew here today—"

"So I see," Sybil commented, for several uniformed maids were busily at work in the living and dining rooms. The sounds of vacuum cleaners vibrated into the hall from the library and game room. "I used to use

Pretty Maid Service, but I found another company much better. You should have asked me for a recommendation."

Ignoring Sybil's critical remarks, she replied, "I think the breakfast room is safe from all the confusion. Why don't you wait there while I run upstairs and tell Melva you're here? I'm sure Mrs. Dietz will be happy to set out some refreshments," she added, not even blinking at the bold-faced lie. Forced to play hostess at such a time stretched Robyn's patience to an explosive limit. She'd only been back from Chataqua for a few minutes and hadn't had time to adjust to all the instant demands.

Without giving them a chance to argue, she turned away and hurried up the stairs to the second floor. After looking in several doorways, she found Melva in a small study off Lynette's master bedroom, supervising one of the cleaners.

"Now, be sure to put everything back in exactly the same place after you dust," Melva instructed. "The lady of the house is kinda particular. Not like me," she hastened to add. "Landsake, I'd never turn my place upside down like this. I don't—" She broke off as Robyn came into the room. "My goodness, what put a glower like that on your face, Robyn?"

"Melva, have you seen Becky? Darrel and Sybil are here."

"Oh, they're back already. Did they bring suitcases with them?"

"What?"

"I was just wondering if they were planning on staying and helping out."

"No," Robyn said with a firmness that didn't allow for any contradiction. "I'm sure they're here to pick up Becky. Where is she?"

Melva thought a minute. "I think she was going to play outside. Ask Mrs. Dietz. Becky was in the kitchen when the cleaning ladies arrived. I've had my hands full supervising the second floor cleaning, but we're almost through here."

"I appreciate your help, Melva. Truly, I do."

"I thought Lynette was going to do something with this room. It's the same unhandy arrangement that Darrel and Sybil put up with when they lived here. Didn't Lynette talk about knocking out a wall and adding this space to her bedroom?"

"Yes, she decided the library served her needs well enough, so she's pretty much ignored this room." Robyn frowned as the cleaning lady was about to open a bookcase to dust a couple of dozen leather-bound volumes.

"Don't bother with those," Robyn said quickly. "There are more pressing needs."

"How about your bedroom?" Melva asked.

"No. I'll keep my door shut. Don't bother with it."

"Good." Melva lowered her voice. "I could almost feel Heather's cold breath on the back of my neck when I peeked in this morning to see if you were there. All of Lynette's decorating hasn't changed the room that much. It'll always be the nursery. I've heard that those who have been wronged in life linger as ghosts to exact their due." She shivered. "It kinda makes you believe in ghosts, doesn't it? I mean, it's been eleven years and

I still have the feeling that Heather is hanging around. This house seems filled with silent secrets, somehow."

I've had the same feeling.

For a moment Robyn wondered if she'd spoken aloud, but Melva's attention had already shifted to the maid, and she was instructing her to move on to the master bedroom.

"If I know Lynette she'll have a fit if there's a speck of dust anywhere." Melva's tone was testy.

"I'll check on Becky," Robyn offered quickly, as if she had nothing better to do at the moment. Although she appreciated Melva's help, looking after the woman's granddaughter wasn't on Robyn's over-crowded agenda.

As she came down the stairs, she saw Mrs. Dietz standing outside on the front steps, and heard her calling Becky's name. "Where is she?" Robyn asked as she joined the housekeeper. She couldn't see any sign of the child on the front lawn or surrounding landscape.

"The gazebo," Mrs. Dietz answered shortly. "At least, that's where she said she was going. She told me she needed an office and the house was too crowded." The woman shrugged her thick shoulders. "Me, I don't ask questions."

"There she is," Robyn said as Becky emerged from the vine-covered structure.

With a start, Robyn saw she wasn't alone. Brian was holding her hand, and Becky was talking earnestly to him as they walked up the sidewalk to the house. Mrs. Dietz muttered something under her breath and disappeared inside.

As they approached the steps, Robyn wondered if

Becky had been in the gazebo earlier when she'd passed it on her way to the house. She hadn't even glanced in that direction, and Becky hadn't made a sound or called out to her. Either Brian had been more perceptive, or the little girl had made her presence known to him.

As Robyn watched them walking together, her chest tightened. She was used to feeling like an outsider, but for some reason there was a deeper sense of loneliness than usual as she recognized a bonding between the man and child. Her pride still smarted from the collapse of the fantasy of her own making. Even now she felt a strange loss for something that had never been. When they reached the steps, she smiled at Becky and ignored Brian. "Honey, your parents arrived a few minutes ago. They're in the breakfast room, waiting to see you. Isn't that a nice surprise?"

Becky's scowl was her wordless answer.

"I bet they brought you back something from their trip." She coaxed, "You'd better run along and see what it is."

With childish stubbornness, Becky answered, "I already know. Something stupid. I had to buy my own detective kit."

Robyn was sure Brian was hiding a smile as he cleared his throat. "Maybe they'll surprise you. You're a lucky girl, Becky. I'll bet they do a lot of things to make you happy."

"Do you think they'll let me stay here until after the party?"

Robyn was about to hedge an answer when Brian

spoke up. "I don't know, Becky, but that cute smile of yours is plenty hard to resist."

She pulled on his hand. "You'll come with me?"

"Sure, I'd like to meet your parents."

AS THE THREE OF THEM went into the house, Brian slipped the play badge into his pocket. He'd been wondering how he was going to arrange contact with Darrel and Sybil Sheldon that wouldn't seem contrived. He welcomed this opportunity, which seemed perfectly natural. Obviously, Becky's plan to solve her own kidnapping wasn't their idea. He'd have to be very careful not to let their daughter jeopardize his situation. If anyone even got a whiff of his interest in the unsolved crimes, he'd never be able to get at the truth.

He glanced at Robyn's closed expression as they headed for the breakfast room. Undoubtedly, the early arrival of the Sheldons only added to the weight of responsibility she was carrying. Her lovely shoulders were squared and her chin set in a determined line.

He wished he could put an arm around her and invite her to rest her head on his shoulder. Better than that, he wished he could take her sailing or dancing. The glimpse he'd had of what lay beneath her outward rigidity intrigued him. He was convinced that under different circumstances getting to know the real Robyn Valcourt would be worth the effort.

Forget that, he told himself. When she learned of his deception he'd be lucky if she ever spoke to him again.

Becky's parents welcomed their daughter with open arms. "How are you, darling? Did you miss us?"

Becky laughed openly when her daddy picked her up and swung her around in a circle. "Papa, this is my new friend," she bubbled, pointing at Brian.

"Nice to meet you, new friend." Darrel smiled as he set Becky down, and held out his hand.

"Brian Keller. Nice to meet you. I'm here for the big celebration."

"Keller. Of course." Darrel nodded. "The Parkers bought the house from Joe Keller, the prizefighter."

"A distant relative. I'm representing the family in his absence. And trying to help out a little getting ready for the big day."

Robyn didn't rise to the opportunity to confirm his helpfulness. Instead, she kept a polite smile on her face and, always the perfect hostess, assured them that Mrs. Dietz would be bringing in some refreshments.

"This is my wife, Sybil," Darrel said.

"Nice to meet you, Mrs. Sheldon," Brian responded politely. Sybil nodded slightly and then gave her attention to smoothing back Becky's hair and tying a dangling ribbon. Brian wondered how she'd handled the kidnapping and the murder of the nursemaid who'd been in charge of her infant daughter. From the woman's cool manner, it wasn't likely he was going to get any easy answers from her.

"We just got back in town this morning," Darrel told Brian. "But we have to leave again for a couple of days in New York."

Becky bounced happily in her chair. "Then Grammie and I can stay here!"

"If it's all right with Robyn," Darrel cautioned.

Brian thought Robyn's hesitation spoke volumes, but Darrel didn't seem to notice. "We'll be back in time for the big bash," he assured her. "I know Mother will want to stay and help."

Melva came in the room in time to hear his remark, and quickly agreed. "There are too many things left to do. Robyn will never get everything done by herself in the short time that's left."

"What about the Koleski family?" Darrel asked. "Anybody from that clan coming?"

Robyn nodded. "Yes, we've heard from two lines of descendants of the original owners. They're scattered all over the country, and from what I've learned they all have big families. I don't have a firm count on how many of them will be here."

A moment later, the sound of a pickup truck coming up the driveway and parking near the side of the house drew everyone's eyes to the window.

"It's Nick," Darrel said. "He's got a load of something."

"I bet he could use some help." Brian quickly rose to his feet. "Maybe it's material for the boathouse repairs."

"What's wrong with the boathouse?" Darrel asked, getting up and following Brian out of the breakfast room.

As they left the house Brian explained about the winter storm, but he could see that the back of the trunk wasn't loaded with building material. It was filled with cases of wine, champagne, soft drinks, bottled water and two kegs of beer.

Nick was squinting at a list in his hands as he eased his long legs out of the cab. Brian thought he still looked strung out from his late night.

"Is somebody having a party?" Darrel quipped as he peered into the truck bed. "There's enough booze here for one lost weekend."

"Took an hour to load," Nick growled, and squinted as if he had a headache. "If I didn't get everything, there'll be hell to pay."

"Want us to give you a hand, Nick?" Brian asked. "Just tell us where all this goes."

"I'm not sure. Oh, here's the boss lady."

Robyn let the screen door slam behind her and came over to the truck. Nick handed her the piece of paper. "Everything's checked off. Right brand and everything."

"Good job, Nick." Robyn sighed with obvious relief. "Grandmother is pretty particular about the quality of food and drink she serves to guests."

"You're telling me! Where do you want all this stuff?" Nick asked. "I'd like to get on it while I've got a couple of strong bucks here willing to help."

"We'll need to divide everything in thirds so we can stock the recreation room, kitchen and boathouse," she told him. "One beer keg goes downstairs and one in the boathouse."

"Okay, I'll load a wheelbarrow and make a couple trips down to the boathouse." Nick turned to Darrel. "Why don't you take the kitchen, and we'll see if good old Brian can handle the basement stairs." He grinned at Brian as if sending him a challenge.

Robyn turned to Darrel. "Ask Mrs. Dietz where to stack the things in the pantry, and I'll show Brian where the recreation room storage is."

Brian was wondering if she was remembering the last time they were together in the rec room.

ROBYN PICKED UP one of the lighter boxes of wine and Brian hoisted a heavy beer keg up on one shoulder. As they quickly descended the basement stairs together, Robyn wondered what Brian thought of her rude behavior in Chatagua. Now that she'd had time to absorb the shock of her earlier eavesdropping, she was, in some ways, already regretting her rather childish reaction.

After all, a handsome, virile man like Brian Keller must have a history of feminine conquests, she told herself. But almost immediately this thought was followed by a surge of fresh determination.

I don't intend to be one of them!

She led the way to a small room that had been designed by the original owners as a fruit cellar. Through the years it had been turned into a small game room, storage room, and now a compact wine cellar.

"Grandmother likes to keep them full," Robyn explained when Brian commented that there were already enough racks of bottles to host a dozen celebrations— not to mention a spare keg of beer. "She's used to giving lavish parties, and can't seem to break some of the habits she acquired as an ambassador's wife."

"I guess it's worth all the effort if you like this sort of thing. I imagine you had some pretty extravagant birthday parties when you were growing up."

"Not really. My parents had so many obligations to fulfill there wasn't much time for family affairs, and when I came to live with Lynette, her social calendar seemed to be just as busy." Robyn turned a speculative gaze on him. "What about you? All I know is that you're a distant relative of Joe Keller. You've never mentioned anything personal about yourself. Are your parents alive? Do you have siblings? A girlfriend or wife?"

"Yes, my parents are alive, and no, I don't have brothers, sisters, girlfriend or wife."

She was about to challenge his statement when John Parker came down the basement steps, calling her name.

"Oh, Mr. Parker," Robyn said, surprised when she saw who it was. The distinguish-looking, gray-haired man stopped in the middle of the recreation room. "We were just replenishing the wine cellar. This is Brian Keller. He's been helping us out."

"Yes, Todd mentioned that Mr. Keller was an early arrival." As if Brian weren't standing there, he centered his attention on Robyn. "I was hoping I could take a pretty lady out to lunch. In fact, I promised Todd we'd meet him at the club, and you wouldn't want to make a liar out of me, would you?"

Robyn almost refused the invitation, and then changed her mind. She could use some pampering. The Parkers weren't her company of choice, but they might be just what she needed to get her emotions back on an even keel.

"Lunch sounds great," she responded, smiling. "I haven't been to the club since I got back. Oh, by the way, the Sheldons are here. I expect they'd like to say hello to you before we leave."

"It's been awhile since I've seen Darrel."

Giving Brian a hurried smile, she said, "Thanks for helping Nick out."

Robyn paused, not knowing what else to say. John Parker was looking at the both of them in a way that made her uncomfortable. Surely he wouldn't read anything into the two of them being alone in the basement.

JOHN PARKER. Had this lawyer friend of his father's recognized him? Brian wondered after he and Robyn had disappeared up the stairs. Maybe dyed hair and a change in physique hadn't been enough to disguise the young kid who had carried his golf clubs on a couple of occasions. Brian was a little relieved that the man's posture and manner had indicated that he'd already classified Brian Keller as unworthy of any cultivation.

Parker had handled the infant adoption for the Sheldons, but all efforts to gain any disclosures about that adoption had failed. The lawyer circumvented any attempt to have information released. He had been one of the sharpest lawyers in the state before his retirement, Brian knew, and was likely as cunning as ever. Since Parker had been the Sheldons' legal counselor, he very likely had information that could open up a new avenue of investigation. How to access that information might be Brian's greatest challenge. In contrast to Melva Sheldon's easy chatter, the lawyer gave every impression that he never uttered a single word without careful consideration. But Brian had dealt with men like him before. Sometimes they were so careful trying to withhold information that they unwittingly earmarked the very things they were trying to conceal.

Brian made a few more trips unloading the pickup, and then decided to check out the rest of the basement. He found a warren of connecting rooms that apparently had served a variety of purposes throughout the years. He came across a huge metal safe that might have been in service during the roaring twenties, when the house was a speakeasy. The door hung open, and only dust and some mouse droppings were inside. Brian wondered if anyone still knew the combination.

Deep in thought, he made his way back upstairs. Only Melva and Becky remained in the small dining room. Assuming that Nick must be in the boathouse, Brian headed that way. When he reached the door there and started up the wrought-iron staircase, he was surprised to hear Sybil Sheldon's voice raised in anger.

Brian stopped before reaching the landing, and listened to her mounting tirade.

"I'm sick of your excuses."

"Oh, give it a rest, Sybil."

"I can't. I keep remembering—"

"Blast it all!" Nick swore. "I don't want to hear any more! The whole thing is over and done with! Heather's dead."

Sybil's voice was suddenly as cold as if icicles dripped from every word. "And I'm going to make sure it's on your conscience until the day you die."

Her footsteps warned Brian in time to retreat down the steps and hide behind some lumber as Sybil passed him. Her vehement words rang in his ears and brought a startling and unexpected perspective.

Was it possible the nursemaid's murder was unrelated to the kidnapping?

AT LUNCH, Robyn found herself totally bored. She did her best to feign interest in dull topics of conversation, but at the back of her mind, the earlier events of the day churned, seeming to mock her. Except for her childish behavior, she could have been having an exciting lunch with Brian. Even if he was lying about not having a girlfriend named Ginger, she could still enjoy his friendly company, and not be sitting here, glancing at her watch.

The exclusive country club overlooked lush greens and fairways of the golf course. Round tables under colorful umbrellas were scattered on a wide veranda bordered by rich plantings of riotous flowers.

If Robyn had been with anybody but the Parkers, she would have opted for sitting outside, but she knew that Todd hated sun, wind and water. He never would have sat on a pier, dangling his legs over the water, watching a fish swim by and— *Stop it! Stop thinking about Brian Keller.*

"What is it, honey?" Todd touched her hand. "What's the matter? You're frowning."

"Am I? Sorry." She forced a smile. "How are you liking your new Porsche?" The question was enough to start Todd on his favorite line of conversation.

The way John Parker beamed at the two of them

made Robyn wish she'd had enough sense not to encourage Todd's attention. When several of Lynette's friends stopped by the table to inquire about her, Robyn was kept busy role-playing the gracious granddaughter.

"Yes, she's attending a wedding in the Bahamas," she said with a practiced smile. "I expect her home shortly before the house celebration."

Surprisingly, John Parker chatted with the ladies, giving them some flattering compliments that brought rosy blushes to their faces. Robyn remembered Lynette had said something about him being something of a rake in his younger years. His wife had passed away a few years ago, but Todd's father had never remarried, and John's sister, Cora, still lived with them. Someone had said his wife and son had never forgiven him for selling Stoneview to the Sheldons.

When the late luncheon was finally over, John Parker declared he had business waiting at his office, and asked Todd to drive Robyn home.

The sunny day had given way to an overcast sky, and the air was heavy with threatening rain clouds. They barely made it back to Stoneview before the storm hit, with forks of lightning warning that a downpour was not far behind.

As they stood in the foyer, Robyn deftly disengaged herself from Todd's guiding arm. "Thanks for lunch. It was a nice break. There're only a few days left to get everything ready before Grandmother gets back. I'll have to keep on my toes to have it all done in time."

"The party was her idea. Why not let her handle it?"

Robyn wasn't going to go there. She quickly changed the subject. "What about the boathouse? I thought the insurance was arranging for some repair-men to get it back in shape?"

"They'll be here tomorrow. I'll come around and check on them." He gave her a smile and invited a kiss, but she moved back.

"I'll see you then…." Her voice trailed off, and she prepared to shut the door after him.

"Robyn, honey, we really need to talk. Why do you keep putting me off?" His tone was more openly de-manding. "Why can't you be up front about things? Just come out with it, for Pete's sake."

"I'm sorry. After the party, we'll talk, I promise."

He just shrugged as if he'd heard that promise before, and left the house, hurrying to his car as the rain began to fall. A clap of thunder warned that more was on the way.

The house was strangely quiet as Robyn walked past shadowy rooms that had been filled with the bustle of the cleaners when she'd left. Her footsteps echoed on the polished plank flooring as she made her way to the back of the house.

Mrs. Dietz was in the kitchen, and she told Robyn that she thought Melva and Becky were in the game room, playing cards.

"What about Nick and Mr. Keller?"

"They're trying to block the open doors of the boat-house before the storm hits. Nick says we're in for some strong winds tonight."

As if on cue, a whipping wind under the eaves of the house created a high-pitched wailing as the rain came down. Outside the kitchen window, branches of nearby red oaks whipped madly, like crazed dancers writhing in the air, and once again an approaching rumbling warned that lightning strikes were getting closer.

Robyn was tempted to stay in the bright kitchen with the housekeeper, but Mrs. Dietz had never encouraged company in her domain.

"Will you be wanting a dinner tray in the library as usual?" she asked briskly as she moved quickly from cupboards to refrigerator.

"Yes, that'll be fine." She knew that Melva and Becky would have their usual evening meal in the small dining room.

After Robyn turned on the lights in the library, she went to the windows to close the drapes, and saw Nick and Brian heading at a fast run toward the cottage.

Was it only that morning that she'd had coffee in the kitchen with them? It seemed like aeons ago. Why had an outing that started out so promising become another lesson in the folly of expectation? Letting her emotions run free had never brought anything but more loneliness.

I'm a slow learner about some things, she admitted to herself as she settled at the desk in front of the computer.

The day's mail waited for her attention, and she quickly thumbed through the pile to sort out the letters. When she came to a plain, small envelope with no return address, she was puzzled. It was postmarked Chataqua and addressed to her, in bulky capital letters.

She slit it open and drew out a torn piece of newspaper. She immediately recognized it as a copy of the society blurb about the celebration. Ugly red letters scrawled over the story leaped out at her: "*WARNING! PARTY OR FUNERAL? CANCEL NOW!*"

She dropped the paper as if it were a poisonous barb. With quickened breath Robyn stared at it. Who would send such a thing? And why would someone address it to her instead of Lynette? What did it mean? And what should she do about it?

Her hands were sweaty as she reached for the phone and called her grandmother without even calculating the time difference. This was one crisis she was not going to handle by herself. Surprisingly enough, her call to the Bahamas went right through, and Lynette answered the phone after only three rings.

"Thank goodness," Robyn breathed when she heard her voice. "I was afraid I wouldn't catch you."

"Robyn? You sound out of breath. What on earth is the matter?" she asked. "Is something wrong?"

As succinctly as she could, Robyn described the ugly message on the newspaper clipping. "What should I do? Call the police and turn it over to them?"

"What?" Her grandmother's voice rose. "Call the police? And have the law all over the house, ruining everything? Don't be ridiculous, Robyn. Don't you see that's what this jealous, spiteful person wants? I knew there would be plenty of noses out of joint when I decided to limit the invitations, but I didn't think anyone would stoop to such childishness. Do nothing! Absolutely nothing." Lynette's authoritative tone brooked no argument. "Don't let anyone know about it. Heavens, if something like this gets out, the publicity would ruin everything. We can't have that, can we?"

Robyn didn't trust herself to respond. She needed time to think.

Lynette didn't seem to notice. "I'll be taking a short cruise with the wedding party to an island where the ceremony is going to take place. Absolutely divine," Lynette bubbled. "Then I'll be home, dear. You sound a little tired. Are you getting enough rest? I've told you to hire all the help you need."

Lynette launched into a recital of instructions Robyn had already heard more than once. She listened to her grandmother's monologue for another five minutes, and then hung up after promising she'd keep silent about the awful threat—for now.

Robyn dropped the venomous letter into a bottom drawer and shut it firmly, as if such a simple act could contain the morbid energies of the ugly warning. She made a decision to tell Nick to hire some extra security for the party weekend.

She knew there had been problems with an intruder when Nick had been getting the property ready for the Valcourts' arrival after the Sheldons had moved out the same year as the crimes. Nick had found evidence that someone had been in the house and on the grounds, so he had moved into the cottage to serve as a watchman. By the time Robyn's grandparents were ready to occupy the estate, they were assured that the premises were secure. There'd never been any cause or concern for the safety of the family or guests—until now!

When Mrs. Dietz brought in the tray, Robyn ate sparingly of the halibut steak, vegetable salad and blueberry tart. After working another hour finalizing the guest list, she called it quits. She might have joined Melva and Becky, but a glance at her watch told her it was past the little girl's bedtime.

As Robyn went down the main hall, she passed the open door of a small parlor that was rarely used. Lynette always referred to the windowless room as the "funeral parlor" because old newspapers had shown the original owner of the house, Karl Koleski, lying in state there. Through the years efforts to change the ambience of the dark paneled room had failed. As Robyn paused in the doorway, a rippling chill ran through her.

Party or funeral?

The threatening words of the ugly note flashed in her mind's eye. The cold chill of the house seemed even more intense than ever before. *But I'm not a scared little girl anymore.* She set her chin, walked past the door and continued on up the stairs to her room.

As peals of thunder followed forks of lightning flashing off the lake like an electric current, Robyn prepared for bed. After a quick shower, which revived her spirits somewhat, she slipped into a pair of silk mandarin pajamas scented with a lavender sachet in her drawer. Peering into the mirror as she creamed her face, she noticed two more tiny freckles announcing their alliance with the russet color of her hair. Her eyes reflected a tired heaviness that seemed to go bone deep.

She sighed as she burrowed down under the summer bedcovers and listened to the peppering rain. As she firmly closed her mind to all the perplexing questions that plagued her, the rigidity of her muscles began to ease, and slowly the fatigue of the day overtook her. Wavering on the edge of sleep, she sank into the blessed state of nothingness.

LESS THAN AN HOUR LATER, her eyes jerked open. Her mouth was dry, her pulse thumping.

What was it? Had she been dreaming?

Streams of rain masked the windowpanes, and watery moonlight was shrouded in dark clouds. The small light on a bedside clock failed to dispel the shadows. When a sharp clap of thunder vibrated in the room, she decided the storm must have awakened her.

As she slipped out of bed and hurried to close the drapes, a blinding shaft of light struck a nearby tree. Its glare lit up the room; a second later a piercing, high-pitched wail sounded behind her.

All the nightmares of her life were centered in that moment. Robyn stood mesmerized as an undefined whiteness floated toward her from a corner of the nursery alcove.

As the vision came closer, the whiteness took form. A white blanket fell away and two plump little arms reached out and clutched her around the waist.

"Becky!"

"I'm scared," she whimpered.

Robyn hugged her and held her close. "It's all right. It's just the storm."

"I don't like it."

"Neither do I. You're cold and shivering. Let's get into bed."

The two of them huddled together under the warm covers.

"That's better," Robyn said as they snuggled close. "You'll be warm as toast in a few minutes," she promised, surprised at how nice it felt to have a cuddling little body sharing her bed.

Becky murmured, "You smell good."

Robyn chuckled silently and gave her a hug. "Thank you. Now, honey, would you like to tell me why you're not in your own bed? What are you doing here?"

"Waiting," Becky answered in a small voice.

"Waiting for what?"

"I don't know," she admitted. "Maybe a ghost? A murderer? I think it's called a stakeout."

Chapter Seven

Robyn was able to slip Becky back into her own bed early the next morning before Melva knew she'd been gone. As Robyn tucked her in, the little girl snuggled against her pillow and closed her eyes for another nap, looking totally angelic. Robyn smiled affectionately and marveled at the child's stubborn determination to pursue her detective game. She was very serious about the whole thing, and Robyn knew that getting her interested in anything else was not going to be easy. Impulsively, she leaned down and laid a light kiss on her forehead.

Then, as if this sudden expression of affection was threatening, she quickly turned and quietly left the room.

The storm had passed, leaving a soggy landscape and a dull gray patina on the lake. Robyn was too wide awake to even think about going back to bed. She quickly dressed in a new pair of designer jeans and a loosely knit pullover top in a variegated blue-and-russet pattern that enhanced her eyes and hair.

Deftly she wove her locks in a French braid and touched her lips lightly with pink gloss. As she turned around to catch her reflection in the tall mirror, she was satisfied that Mrs. Dietz's relentless offering of rich food had not settled in her hips. The housekeeper was nowhere to be seen in the kitchen, and Robyn happily put on a pot of coffee. She was taking some Danish pastries out of the freezer when she glanced out the back window and glimpsed someone in a thick stand of tall oak trees near the driveway.

Brian! Why was he wandering around in that area of the grounds so early in the morning? Quietly opening the back door, she stood watching him as he paused at the edge of the grove, bent his head back and looked upward.

As she followed his gaze, she saw what had captured his interest. The tallest of the trees was newly charred and black. It must have been the one struck by lightning at the height of last night's storm.

Letting the screen door bang behind her, she hurried down the steps, and as she walked over to where he stood, his face registered surprise. He took his hands out of the pockets of the light windbreaker he wore and smiled at her.

"Well, good morning. I thought I was the only one up and about this early," he stated. "I was curious to see how close that lightning strike came last night."

"That was some show, wasn't it?"

"Look at that scorched tree. It's a blessing the rain prevented this whole stand from catching fire. It would have been a shame to lose all these trees—and threaten the house as well. I circled the house and saw spots where some digging had been done. Some looked fairly recent."

"Nick has a gardener who was probably taking out some undergrowth or planting something."

"I didn't see any signs of other lightning strikes."

"Thank goodness."

As the memory of the storm and the fright Becky had given her swept back, Robyn realized with surprise that she wanted to share the incident with Brian. His affection for the little girl was obvious, and he'd understand Robyn's concern for the lengths Becky was willing to go to pursue this fixation of hers.

"Would you like a fresh cup of coffee? I just made a pot." She could tell the invitation took him by surprise. "We'll have the kitchen all to ourselves this early."

"Sounds great."

THEY WALKED BACK to the house, and Robyn quickly set out some cups on a small table in a nook in a corner of the kitchen. As he watched her, he wondered why her chill of yesterday had been replaced by this offering of friendship.

She had shed her lady-of-the-manor persona for the moment, and the soft curve of her lips and her smooth forehead were a pleasant surprise. The memory of her laughter and sparkling eyes on the boat ride brought a fresh flush of pleasure. The sweetness of that brief kiss lingered and certainly created a temptation for more, but too much depended upon her acceptance of his presence in and around the house. He didn't want to foul up his investigation.

He let her set the subject of conversation, and he didn't have to wait long before he found out the reason she'd invited him for coffee.

"It's Becky," she said as she poured the freshly brewed coffee and offered him a strawberry-cream pastry.

"Oh, what's our budding Nancy Drew been up to now?"

Robyn took another sip of coffee as if trying to collect the right words to express herself. Then she set down her cup and looked him directly in the face. "This detective game has gotten out of hand. For the child's sake we've got to stop it before she hurts herself."

"What has Becky been up to now?"

Brian was surprised at her affectionate tone as she told him what had happened. He managed to keep a straight face over the "stakeout" remark.

Obviously Robyn had been shaken by the child's ghostlike appearance. "I'm sorry she frightened you," he said, impulsively reaching over to cover her free hand with his. "You're right. Wandering around in the middle of the night is not a good idea."

She withdrew her hand as if startled by the physical contact. "Digging up the past doesn't do anyone any good. Don't you agree?"

He took a sip of coffee before replying. In fact, he admired the child's stubborn determination to try and find out the truth of the near tragedy of her infancy. He thought about his father's pain over the scandal that had unfairly tarnished his reputation, and he wondered how Robyn would react if he leveled with her that his rapport with Becky lay in a shared commitment. He wanted to say that some things needed to be brought to light so they could be laid to rest, but he didn't.

"I'll talk to her," he promised.

"Good. She's seems to have bonded with you. And I don't think she'll listen to me. I've never been very good with kids. I grew up in an adult world where behavior and manners were everything. I think I was role-playing at being adult from the time I could walk and talk."

"That's too bad. Some of my fondest memories are of splashing barefoot through mud puddles or jumping out of bushes scaring everyone with a water snake."

She chuckled and shook her head. "I can tell you're not going to be very good at keeping Becky on the straight and narrow.

"No wonder you two hit it off so well. Two peas in a pod, for sure."

"I'll try to get her sidetracked," he promised. He didn't want Becky upsetting Robyn, and he didn't want the little girl bumbling around, making his investigation any more difficult than it was.

As they compared reminiscences of childhood holidays and events, a hint of friendship seemed to be developing. Even as Brian felt Robyn reaching out to him, he imagined the bitter censure that would be in her eyes when she found out he had been feeding her lies from the beginning. But he couldn't tell her the truth if he hoped to clear his father's name. Not yet.

When Mrs. Dietz came bustling into the kitchen a few minutes later, she was obviously displeased to find squatters in her domain. She tried to shoo them into the breakfast room by offering to fix them a "decent" breakfast, but neither Robyn nor Brian accepted her offer.

They were leaving the kitchen when Nick came in the side door and met them in the hall. "There you are," he greeted Brian. "I heard you leaving without breakfast."

"I was curious to see if there was any damage from the storm."

"No need for you to check it out. I'd take care of it soon enough." Nick didn't bother to hide his irritation.

"I was just curious," Brian explained quickly. *Ouch. He'd stepped on Nick's toes without meaning to.*

"So was I," Robyn said smoothly. "Let's hope that's the last bad weather until after the party. Oh, by the way, Nick, I talked to my grandmother last night. She wants you to hire a couple of security guards for the event."

"Security guards? What the hell for? Is she expecting some gate crashers?"

Brian watched the color drain from Robyn's face as she answered rather sharply, "Well, let's hope not."

"Then why bother with extra muscle all over the place?"

"I never question my grandmother's decisions," she answered stiffly.

Brian didn't believe her. He was good at reading faces, and he was positive she was hedging. If Robyn was arranging for extra security, she darn well knew why.

Nick mumbled something under his breath. "I guess I could hire a couple of bouncers that work at Al's Pub. Damned if I know what they'll do with themselves at a shindig like this. Ain't likely they'll toss some 'fancy pants' out on his butt for drinking too much champagne."

"Just do it, Nick," Robyn ordered. "And I want them on duty the night before the celebration."

He scowled. "Anything else?"

"We're going to need to bring suitable chairs from the second floor rooms to put in the drawing room," she replied. Nick's tone was less than cordial, but Robyn seemed to ignore it. "Lynette doesn't want to use folding chairs in there. There are at least two tapestry chairs in my grandmother's sitting room, and a couple in the front guest bedroom."

"I can handle that," Brian volunteered, hoping he didn't seem too willing. But he'd been looking for an excuse to get upstairs so he could check the attic for anything that might have been stored there when the Sheldons sold the house.

Robyn gave him a grateful smile. "I'd appreciate it."

Nick mumbled something about working outside and cleaning up the debris that blew in from the storm. "I hope those high winds didn't wreck the boathouse repairs. The insurance workmen are supposed to come today and stay until they finish."

Robyn visibly squared her shoulders. "The catering company will be sending out people today to decorate the tables and arrange the place settings. I'll be overseeing the preparations." Looking at Brian directly, she said, "Let me know how things go, will you?"

"Sure thing."

He knew she wasn't referring to moving chairs. She wanted an update on his talk with Becky. At the moment, he had no idea how he was going to sidetrack such a persistent, stubborn but purposeful little girl.

After Robyn had left them, Nick audibly muttered a few swear words about having to hire security guards.

"Damn foolishness. Is she expecting some high-falutin' society brawl? Doesn't make sense."

Brian had to agree. This birthday party was supposed to be a happy get-together of families who had shared living on a lovely estate over a hundred-year period. Why was Lynette Valcourt expecting trouble?

"Has there been any vandalism since you've been here?" Brian asked casually.

"Nope. While I was getting the Sheldons settled in their new place, and the Valcourts hadn't move in here yet, there were reports of a prowler on the grounds. A basement window had been broken, but the police didn't find any evidence of looting. After that incident, Lynette put in a security system that would guard Fort Knox."

"And you've never seen anybody suspicious hanging around?"

"Not since the Valcourts moved in," he answered flatly.

"How about when you worked for the Sheldons?"

His jaw clenched visibly. "No, I never saw anyone, but after what happened to Heather, I wished I'd paid attention to the feeling I had that someone was sneaking around. A few times I patrolled the grounds but didn't see anybody."

"Who do you think it might have been?"

"Who in hell knows?" he snapped. "Don't you think I've asked myself that a hundred times?"

Brian nodded. "I'm sure you have."

The man's emotions seemed sincere, but the reason for them could be suspect. What if they were based in jealousy and remorse? For the second time, Brian considered the possibility that Heather's death might be unrelated to the kidnapping.

"Anyway, who's going to need guards at a shindig like this?" Nick growled as they left the house and returned to the cottage to get ready for the day's work.

Brian wondered the same thing. Something had motivated Lynette to hire extra security. What? He knew his chances of getting the answers from her granddaughter were slight. Obviously, family business was not something Robyn would readily share.

When they reached the cottage, Nick called several telephone numbers before he had lined up his "security team"—a couple of fellows who had proved themselves as bouncers at Al's Pub and Grill.

"This is a hoity-toity affair, not some tavern bash," he warned them. "Dress decent." After he hung up, he shook his head and told Brian, "I don't know if either of them have a spare pair of jeans, let alone any fancy clothes."

"Why didn't you call a security company and hire a couple of professionals?"

"'Cause I don't want any stiff-necked security guards thinking they can run things." He scowled. "I'm boss here, and that isn't going to change just 'cause the old woman wants to show off."

"Is that what's she's doing?"

"What else? She wants all them ritzy gals thinking their jewelry is protected while they're waltzing around all over the place. Security guards, my foot! What a crock."

"Maybe you're right," Brian answered, but he suspected it was something more than that.

After Nick collected garden tools to rake and bag the debris left by the wind and rain, he left the cottage, slamming the door behind him. Brian wondered if there was some other reason he didn't want professional security guards wandering around. Maybe Nick had more than a signed photo hidden somewhere.

BRIAN RETURNED to the mansion, pleased that he had a reason to disappear upstairs and check out the second floor and attic. As he came in the side door, he saw that Melva and Becky had just come downstairs. There was no way he could pass the breakfast room without saying hello.

Becky was slumped over her bowl of cereal, her head resting in one hand, and she barely glanced up at Brian when he came in. Melva, on the other hand, was her usual spritely self.

"Sit yourself down, and try some biscuits and sausage gravy," she invited, waving at a chair next to her.

He hesitated a split second before deciding not to pass up the opportunity to see if Melva might shed some light on Lynette's need for increased security.

"Smells good. I think I will."

Quickly, he served himself a plate from the sideboard. After all, coffee and a pastry didn't count as breakfast, and hauling chairs all over the house was going to take energy. Since he'd promised Robyn to have a talk with Becky, he hoped Melva might say something about the girl's nightly prowl that could lead into a lecture by both her grandmother and him.

However, after a few minutes of idle chatter, it soon

became apparent to Brian that Melva didn't know her granddaughter had been out of her bed during the storm. His repeated attempts to draw Becky into the conversation were only reciprocated with some one-syllable mutterings or shrugs. Obviously this wasn't the time for any kind of persuasive dialogue with the stubborn little girl.

"I heard Nick's hiring some security guards for the celebration," he mentioned casually, hoping to open the door for Melva's input on the subject.

"Landsake, are some of us going to be bounced out on our ear if we drink too much?" She laughed deeply as she raised one eyebrow. "You have to be kidding."

"Nope. Lynette's worried about something?" He phrased it as a question.

"Well, she is going to have a bunch of strangers wandering around. I mean, she doesn't know anything about the Koleski descendants who are coming, and she invited relatives of the other four families. Maybe she's afraid somebody will wander off with some of her treasures."

"Could be. I can't think of any other reason, can you?" he asked, watching her carefully for any slight lowering of eyelids, a tightening around the mouth, a quick glance to one side—all perceptible signs of lying.

"I never try to outguess Lynette. She's one sharp lady." Melva's smile remained in place, and as far as Brian could tell she had no idea why the guards had been hired.

"Maybe she's scared someone will find the bag of money before I do," Becky piped up. "Nobody knows what happened to it."

Melva groaned. "Child...child."

Becky's eyes were bright and snapping. All signs of listlessness were gone. Brian saw the pugnacious jut to her chin, and he was at a loss how to handle the situation. He took the coward's way out and decided to postpone his lecture until a more appropriate time.

As he pushed back from the table, he said, "Well, I'd better collect some chairs for the drawing room. I'll see you two ladies later."

Once upstairs, he located the master suite and adjoining study—a luxurious sitting room, bedroom and private bath that looked like a spread in a decorating magazine. He searched the room and the only thing of interest to his trained eye was a wall safe artfully hidden behind an original French Impressionist painting.

He wondered if the safe had been there when the Sheldons owned the house. Nick had said that Lynette upgraded the security system when she moved in. Was the lady suddenly worried about the safe's contents because of the large number of strangers who would be roaming around the house? Or was her concern based on something entirely different?

Brian made three trips downstairs with chairs, and delayed making the fourth one because he wanted to check out the attic while he had the chance.

No one was in the upper hall as he made his way to the attic door and quietly hurried up the narrow steps. The cavernous storage area seemed darker than the time he'd helped Nick with the folding chairs. The only muted light in the room came through the dormer windows as lingering gray clouds masked the morning sun.

Dare he gamble by turning on an overhead light?

Nick's sharp eyes might register the glow if he happened to glance up at the house. No, better not chance it. Brian had a small pocketlight that would serve to illuminate printing on any of the boxes, and the contents inside.

As he moved farther into a crowded part of the room, his ears caught a faint sound coming from near one of the windows. At first he thought it might be a pane of glass leaking water from the roof. A second sound was more like something alive moving.

Rodents?

Stealthily he moved forward and flashed his small light into the space between the window and the stored boxes and barrels.

"How'd you know where I was?" Becky asked, frowning.

"I didn't," Brian managed to reply, trying to mask his surprise.

She sat among a pile of toys, books, knickknacks, music boxes, rubber balls, a china doll and a couple of stuffed animals. "Look at all the things I found. There's lots more. I only took the stuff I liked."

He nodded in approval. *Problem solved.* Nothing like a bunch of new toys to keep her occupied. "You'll have plenty of fun playing with all of those."

"It's all right, isn't it?" Her wide brown eyes searched Brian's face. "Is someone going to yell at me for taking them?"

"Nope. And if they do just send them to me." He winked. "I'll take care of them."

"I like you," she said with childish honesty. "You understand kids."

The compliment was a startling one because he'd always thought he wasn't very good at relating to children. In fact, he felt a little awkward around them, and it surprised him that somehow Becky had slipped easily into his affections.

"Well, you've made quite a haul. You'd better let me help you carry it down to your bedroom," he said, a little self-conscious under her adoring gaze.

With their arms loaded, they made their way down the attic steps to the second floor. Fortunately, no one was in the hallway, and they reached Becky's room without having to explain themselves.

"Just put everything on the floor by the bed," she told Brian, and began shoving the items she'd been carrying under it.

Brian got the idea. Becky wasn't going to chance her grandmother sending anything back up to the attic. With all that was going on in the house, it wasn't likely anyone would vacuum the floor or peek under the bed before it was time for her to leave with her parents.

"Don't snitch on me."

"Mum's the word," he promised. "Have fun."

With a chuckle, he left her sitting on the floor, holding a stuffed toy and listening to a music box that had two birds chirping away in a gilded cage.

As Brian made his way back to the attic, he hoped Robyn wasn't wondering why he was taking so long bringing down the last chair. She'd be pleased to know that Becky's attention had been diverted—at least for the moment.

The attic was well organized, if such was possible

with all the sundry discards. Household items like dishes were stored in boxes next to fruit jars, outdoor cooking equipment and old pantry food containers. All kinds of clothing hung in old wardrobes or were packed in labeled boxes. Shelves along one wall contained books, newspapers and old catalogs. Athletic equipment and gym lockers were crowded together amid old bicycles and playground equipment. Fishing poles, volleyballs, badminton sets and some warped tennis rackets verified that various occupants of the house had indulged in a variety of pastimes.

Several pieces of white nursery furniture that might have been left behind by the Sheldons caught Brian's attention. He'd hoped that whoever had packed away Heather's belongings might have stored some of them, since she had no family to claim them.

He quickly checked drawers and several boxes, but found only a couple of small poetry books with Heather's name in them. Brian stuck them in his pocket for further examination. None of the rest of the miscellaneous items had any visible connection to the murdered nursemaid.

He was covered with dust when he finally admitted defeat and gave up his search for anything in the attic that would give him some insight into the two crimes. He had to find some bit of evidence soon or his investigation would die a quick death.

Chapter Eight

Robyn was in the front hall talking on the telephone when Brian came downstairs with the last chair.

"Damn!" She swore in unladylike fashion as she replaced the receiver, and ran an agitated hand across her forehead.

"What's wrong?" he asked, searching her haunted eyes.

"That was my landlord. My campus town house suffered water damage in a gale last night. I have to make a trip into Portland and see what needs to be done." She glanced at her wristwatch. "It's a two-hour drive. If I leave now I can make it before lunch."

"I'll go with you."

"Why?" She stared at him, obviously puzzled by the offer.

"You might need to move some things. Maybe I can help. I could even drive and let you relax a little on the way." He could tell that this latest complication was putting her on overload.

After a slight hesitation, she nodded. "Well, if you don't mind."

"Not at all."

"I'll have to make sure everything keeps moving here while I'm gone. Give me about twenty minutes and I'll meet you in the garage. The blue Mustang is mine. I just filled the gas tank. Everything else should be okay. I've only had it out a few times since I've been home."

"Good. I'll see you in twenty minutes."

It was more like forty. Brian would have backed the car out of the garage but he didn't have the keys. Sitting behind the wheel waiting, he was pleased at this unexpected opportunity to touch base with Detective Frank Corelli, who had briefly been his partner in Augusta before transferring to the Portland office. Frank was the only one who knew Brian had revived the Sheldon Cold Case.

When Brian filled him in earlier on his plans, Frank had agreed to keep Brian's undercover status a secret, and had requested the official files on the Sheldon case so he could relay to Brian anything that might not have been followed up during the original investigation. As soon as Brian had a chance in Portland, he'd call him on his cell phone and see if Frank had an update.

"Sorry," Robyn exclaimed as she slipped into the passenger seat and tossed him the keys. "Thanks for driving. I hate city traffic, especially when I have two dozen other things on my mind. I left Melva and Mrs. Dietz with instructions a mile long. I just hope the table decorations are what my grandmother ordered."

"And if they're not? Is there a scaffold for hanging somewhere on the estate?" he teased as he backed out of the garage and turned on to the access road behind the property.

She laughed a little sheepishly. "I guess I do get too worked up trying to be everything my grandmother wants me to be."

"And what exactly is that?"

"Everything she is, I guess." She added wryly, "Sometimes I think she's done her best to clone me." She leaned her head back against the seat. "I don't know. Somewhere along the line I think the real Robyn Valcourt got lost."

"That's too bad. I'd really like to meet her sometime."

She answered softly, "So would I."

"What's holding you back? What would you like to be and do with your life?"

"That's the problem. I'm not sure. I'm good at languages, and I enjoy teaching, but I think I'd like to change schools. Live somewhere else."

"Then why don't you do it?"

"I've thought about it," she admitted.

"Well, that's a start," he said with an encouraging smile.

The highway to the Atlantic Coast was a pleasant drive through blueberry fields and heavily wooded stands of birch, oak and conifers. The sky was still gray and hazy after the storm, and the moist air was redolent with pine scent. Traffic was thin until they approached Portland.

Brian had enjoyed school trips visiting Portland's museums and art galleries, and had enjoyed boat excursions on the water, but he wasn't terribly familiar with the layout of the streets.

Robyn directed him to the western area of the city,

a high promontory where Horizon Women's College was located. Redbrick buildings with gray roofs and long, narrow windows bordered a central expanse of grass and trees. Summer school was in session. Young women dressed in summer clothing dotted the campus. Robyn explained that the college catered to foreign students from all over the world.

"The dean wanted me to teach this summer, but Grandmother had a different idea how I was going to spend my time. My own plans to spend it at our beach house got scuttled."

"I can't imagine Stoneview without you." The truth of his words startled him, and the searching look Robyn gave him demanded an honesty he couldn't give. He changed the subject as he maneuvered through deep puddles and around broken tree limbs and piles of fallen leaves. "They must have had quite a storm here last night, too."

"The faculty town houses are a block away," Robyn told him. "They're owned by the college, and about twenty members of the teaching staff rent them."

The buildings were all painted the same gray-blue, with white shutters. As Brian steered the car into Robyn's garage, it was obvious that the built-in, open-storage bin at the far end had been soaked with rain pouring through a broken windowpane. There was water several inches deep on the floor.

Robyn swore aloud as she viewed drenched suitcases, boxes of books, pictures and a sundry collection of things she had stored there.

"Maybe it's not as bad as it looks," Brian murmured reassuringly.

For the next hour they sorted out everything salvage-able and put everything else in garbage bags. Brian could tell that a lot of the ruined items must have been keepsakes from her years of living abroad with her parents.

There was a tightness to Robyn's lips as she tossed the last plastic sack in a garbage bin behind the building. "Well, that does it. One way to get rid of the past, I guess."

The boxes and other objects she'd set to one side, she asked him to pack in the car. "Thank heavens they escaped water damage. They're things that belong at our summer cottage at Deerpoint. I promised Grandmother I'd see that they got there, but haven't done it. We'll have to drop them off after lunch. Deerpoint is a short drive up the coast."

"Sure." Brian nodded. "No problem."

Glancing at her watch, she said, "It's way past lunch-time. I'm sorry. I bet you're starved."

"Well, my stomach is talking to me," he admitted. "Let's find a good restaurant and enjoy ourselves." He wanted to delay their departure long enough to check in with Corelli.

Robyn hesitated. "I don't know. It's summertime and everything will be crowded."

He suspected she'd been thinking along the lines of a quick sandwich on the way back, so he gave her his best persuasive smile. "Can't you just imagine a steaming lobster bisque, an ocean view and a carafe of white wine?"

"I really should get back," she protested softly.

"Haven't you ever played hooky from school?" he teased.

She shook her head a little regretfully. "Never."

"What a shame...a terrible, terrible shame."

"You're a fake, you know that," she said, laughing at his sad, pathetic look. "But a persuasive fake. All right. Let me check my closet and see if I left anything here that's wearable. I should have rolled up my jeans the way you did. I'm soaked to the skin."

She disappeared into the bedroom, and Brian stepped outside, used his cell phone and quickly called his answering machine. There was only one short message, from Ginger. She'd interviewed one of Heather Fox's friends at the nursing school, but hadn't gleaned any new information. The girl had lost track of Heather after they graduated.

Brian had just stepped back into the house when Robyn appeared, wearing an outfit completely alien to her usual style of dressing. A short floral skirt ended just above her knees, accenting her trim figure and shapely legs. A white peasant blouse dipped provocatively over her full breasts. A gold hair band held back her tumbling shoulder-length, chestnut-colored hair.

Brian's expression must have revealed his surprise because she quickly explained, "I took all my summer clothes to Stoneview with me. This was the only outfit left. I wore it to one of our college shindigs."

"I like it," he said, thinking that if clothes really did make a person, he was pleased how the outfit seemed to change the proper Miss Valcourt.

"I doubt I'll meet any of Grandmother's friends and shock them speechless," she said as they got in her car.

"And who cares?"

"Right. Who cares?" she echoed.

He grinned in approval. If things were different, and he had the time, he might have been able to change her into a real renegade.

"I do have to stop by the college administration office and sign an insurance claim. It shouldn't take but a few minutes," she assured him as they drove away from the town house.

Following her directions, he parked in front of a two-storied brick building. As soon as she disappeared through one of the white double doors, he took out his cell phone again and dialed Corelli's number.

"Frank, it's Brian. I've got just a few minutes—do you have anything for me?"

"Well, not much. The investigation was pretty inclusive. As far as the reports go, there was only one possible lead that never panned out. Karl Koleski, a great-great-grandson of Hugo Koleski, who built Stoneview, was determined to buy the estate when John Parker decided to sell it. Karl's was the highest bid, but for some unknown reason, Parker chose to sell Stoneview to the Sheldons. Disappointed and furious, Karl Koleski harassed the Sheldons in every way possible, was even arrested a couple of times, and vowed revenge. When the Sheldons' baby was kidnapped, the investigator's attention centered on Koleski, but they couldn't break his alibi."

"Where is this Karl Koleski now?"

"His relatives say he's traveling. They claim he has no visible means of support and don't know what he's using for money."

"Somebody must have picked up the ransom. Maybe Karl got even with the Sheldons, but still wants Stoneview," Brian speculated.

"Could be. I got the impression that his side of the family is worried he may show up at the birthday party and ruin everything." Frank lowered his voice. "You'd better be prepared for something more than lighting candles and singing 'Happy Birthday.'"

"I owe you one, Frank."

"Take care, buddy."

"Always."

AS ROBYN WAITED impatiently for a secretary to locate the proper forms, she chided herself for letting Brian talk her into having lunch at the beach. She knew better. Not only was she being irresponsible about giving in to her feelings when she was with him, but she was neglecting her duties by dallying in Portland.

As she left the building, several students stopped to speak to her, obviously surprised to see her dressed so casually. Their eyes followed her as she climbed into the car with Brian. She silently groaned, knowing that an efficient campus grapevine would spread the news: *Miss Valcourt is having a torrid summer romance with a handsome, dark-haired lover.*

"Is something the matter?" Brian asked as they drove away.

"No. Everything's fine." She took a deep breath. "Just fine."

"Good. Let's keep it that way."

"Do you think we can?"

She wondered why his hands tightened slightly on the steering wheel before he assured her, "Of course we can."

The historic area along the water had a unique flavor. Inviting shops, bars and restaurants lined its narrow streets. Robyn loved the brick facades of buildings reflecting the Victorian era. Strangely enough, she'd often felt a kinship with the women of that day. In many ways, Robyn had let her life become as rigid and controlled as Victorian ladies who endured the constraints of a tight corset. Maybe it was her appearance, or the man at her side, that made her suddenly feel free and adventuresome.

"What are you smiling about?" Brian asked as they left the car in a parking lot.

"Just fantasizing. You wouldn't understand. It's a woman thing."

"You look a little rebellious."

"Do I? Maybe it's the company I keep."

"Uh-oh," he said with mock concern. "Am I going to get blamed for any cracks in that proper shell of yours?"

"Absolutely."

He took her hand. "All right, I'm game. Where do you want to eat?"

The restaurant Robyn chose was not one with white tablecloths, hovering waiters and menus printed on ivory parchment. She'd attended college faculty affairs held in most of the elite restaurants near the water, but she'd always envied the student college crowd that frequented more colorful eating places.

The Nautical Warehouse was one of them. She ignored Brian's raised eyebrow as they entered the barnlike building on a pier extending out over the water. The open-beam, high ceiling and rough wooden walls harmonized with copper-topped tables and a bar that looked as if it could offer any drinker his favorite brew or colorful cocktail.

The place seemed to be rocking the pier. Waiters dressed like crewmen off a shrimp boat balanced loaded trays above their heads. At one end of the room was a dance floor, and musicians dressed as pirates were pleasing a vacation crowd of dancers with an upbeat, lively music.

Robyn had heard her students talk about the good times they'd had at the Warehouse, and some of the tales had made her secretly blush. She would never have gone there on her own, and felt a little self-conscious following a bare chested, tattooed maître d' in low-slung jeans as he seated them at a table near the dance floor.

A scantily dressed barmaid immediately sashayed up to the table to take their drink order, and instead of asking for her usual glass of white wine, Robyn heard herself say, "Gin and tonic."

Brian ordered a light beer, and she caught the twinkle in his eyes as he leaned back in his chair. "Nice place, Miss Valcourt. Do you come here often?"

"All the time," she lied.

While they waited for their food and sipped their drinks, the loud music discouraged much conversation. She was surprised when Brian suddenly stood up and held out his hand.

"I think they're playing our song," he said, drawing her to her feet.

Laughing, she followed him out on the dance floor and leaned into his body with remembered pleasure. A romantic ballad invited a closeness that hadn't been there when they had jitterbugged. She felt his warmth invading her as she rested her cheek against him and his hand on her back held her close.

The clamor of laughter, talking and blaring music seemed to reach her ears in muted tones. As if they were alone, cut off from all confusion and harassment, she gave herself up to sensations that excited a desire completely foreign to her.

As she swayed in his arms, his virile, muscular body moving with hers, she tried to deny the sensual demands sluicing through her. By the time the song ended, and they stood looking at each other, she knew she had lost the battle.

When Brian lightly brushed her lips with his, as he had done on the boat, she knew with unequivocal certainty that she wanted more, much more. She didn't care if he had a girlfriend. He was here with her, and that was enough—for now.

He kept his arm around her as they returned to their table, and lunch passed in a kind of haze. The food was excellent. Brian gallantly kept the conversation moving, but an overwhelming question kept stabbing at Robyn. How had it happened? She'd only spent a few days in his company. What did she really know about Brian Keller? How could she have fallen for him?

Her grandmother would absolutely hit the roof.

And what was even stranger, Robyn didn't give a damn about what anyone thought.

THE VALCOURTS' OCEAN HOME, built of natural wood and fashioned with wide decks on both floors, stood on a slight rise overlooking Deerpoint Beach. Robyn much preferred it to Stoneview, and was glad a year-round caretaker kept the house ready for occupancy at a moment's notice. As Brian pulled the car into the driveway, no one would have guessed that the place had been closed up for more than a month.

"I'd planned to spend most of June here, but preparing for the birthday party has kept me at Stoneview," Robyn said as they mounted a set of curved stone steps to the door.

When they entered a long living room, Brian paused in front of a series of picture windows facing the ocean. "What a beautiful view."

The midday sun had burned off the morning's fog, and small islands could be seen dotting the eastern horizon. Even inside the house, the roar of the surf echoed like an orchestral overture, building to a climatic crescendo with the incoming tide.

Robyn was tempted to slip her hand into his as they stood looking at the view. A strange kind of harmony radiated between them, until he abruptly turned away from the windows.

Without looking at her, he said, "I'd better bring those boxes in from the car."

She matched his abrupt tone. "I'll unlock the back door. Better to bring them through the garage. We can stack them in the storeroom off the kitchen."

"I'll take care of it." He disappeared out the front door.

After Robyn had unlocked the back door, she

returned to the living room. There was a chill in the house from last night's storm, and she was pleased to see the fireplace was set for a fire.

By the time Brian finished bringing in the boxes, flames flickered greedily over the dry logs in the fireplace, and Robyn was sitting cross-legged on a plush hearth rug, her face and figure burnished by the golden light.

He mentally groaned as the building sexual hunger that had ignited between them on the dance floor surged through him. Should he turn away before temptation weakened his resolve to keep their relationship safely platonic? The slowly emerging self-confidence and seductive femininity he'd witnessed in Robyn could easily be shattered when she found out his true identity and the deception he'd been playing.

As if she sensed his presence, she turned around. Her lovely lips parted in a welcoming smile. "The fire's wonderful. Come join me."

As he eased down on the rug beside her, dancing glints from the flames were reflected in her eyes, and a rosy glow touched her lips and cheeks. In some ways, he felt as if he were really seeing her for the first time.

"There's something magical about a fire, isn't there," she said, turning her gaze back to the burning logs. "Somehow it's easy to relax and dream as the dancing flames weave a spell. What are your dreams, Brian?" she asked softly.

He kept his gaze on the fire, searching for an answer. He'd been short on dreams for a long time. Life had become too real. Too pragmatic. Sometimes even too ugly for him to do anything but distance himself from it.

"What? No dreams?" she coaxed, when he didn't answer.

"Well, let's see. Once, a long time ago, I thought it would be great to search for sunken treasure." He chuckled at the memory. "I even wrote to a couple of salvage companies, but they didn't answer. I don't know why I even pursued the idea."

"Maybe you were a pirate in another life," she mused, turning to look at him. "Yes, I can see you as a brigadier captain, handsome and fearless, rescuing an unhappy damsel from her dreary life."

"That's a nice story," he said softly. "Especially if the damsel is as lovely as you."

"You think I need rescuing?"

He gently tipped up her chin and searched her shining eyes. "Do you?"

"Yes, please." Her lips were soft and welcoming.

How could he turn away from her now? Things had gone too far, too quickly, he realized. The very air seemed to crackle with unleashed passion as he kissed her.

Not a light brushing of lips. His mouth captured hers with a questing force that banished all pretense between them. Slowly, his hands caressed her breasts and traced the supple smoothness of her body. She responded with an urgency that surprised him. He knew this was not a casual response on her part.

Maybe it was the pirate fantasy that held him back. He touched her eyelids and forehead with his lips, and whispered, "Not now, my beauty. We still have seas to sail."

At first she seemed to be unsure of what was happening. Then, as he continued to hold her close, stroking her hair and pressing a kiss to her forehead, she smiled and seemed to accept the truth of his words.

IT WAS AFTER DARK by the time they headed back to Stoneview. Robyn sat cozily beside Brian in the car as the miles sped by. She'd been looking out the window when she began chuckling.

"What's so amusing?" he asked.

She turned to face him. "What if we don't go back to Stoneview? What if we just send our regrets?"

"You mean ditch the celebration?"

"Everything's almost ready. What could go wrong?"

"Call me a coward, but I'm not up to challenging your grandmother's fury. Only three days left," he reminded her, with a worried edge to his voice that he couldn't quite disguise.

"What's the matter? Do you have to be somewhere?"

He didn't know quite how to answer, so he hedged, "Not really." Even if he stayed longer at Stoneview, remaining undercover wasn't feasible, and once she knew that he'd never in fact been an invited guest, she'd show him the door in quick fashion. Besides, he had obligations to continue his responsibilities with the Boston police department.

When they pulled into the garage at Stoneview, there wasn't any light on in the cottage. Nick must be gone, Brian thought. He'd probably taken advantage of Robyn's absence and headed for Al's Pub and Grill. Brian was disappointed, because he was anxious to find out if Nick had any information about Karl Koleski.

"Wait. I'll walk you to the house," he told Robyn.

"No need. I know the way. I'd rather say goodbye here." She surprised him by giving him a lingering kiss on the lips. Then she turned away quickly and disappeared into the shadows of the overhanging trees planted along the walk.

Brian headed in the opposite direction, toward the cottage. He was only halfway there when Robyn's scream cut through the air like a knife.

Calling her name, he streaked toward the back of the house. When the porch light came into view, he saw her. She was standing at the bottom of the back stairs, shivering and staring up at the screen door.

A huge dark funeral wreath hung there.

The flowers and leaves were dead.

DEATH AT STONEVIEW was printed on a tattered black banner.

Chapter Nine

"What in the hell—?" Brian swore.

"It's the clipping!"

"What clipping?" He could tell from Robyn's expression that she was horrified and frightened.

Her voice wavered. "In the library. I'll show you."

Holding her ice-cold hand, he firmly guided her around the path to the front door. He had no idea what she was talking about. He would come back later and take a closer look at the hideous wreath.

She was trembling so hard when they reached the front that she almost dropped the keys. Brian took them from her, unlocked the door and put a reassuring arm around her shoulders as they entered the shadowy house.

As usual, a hushed, echoing silence was only broken by their footsteps as they made their way down the hall to the library.

"It's all right," Brian lied as he tried to soothe her.

Robyn headed straight for her desk after they'd turned on an overhead light. Jerking open a bottom drawer, she took out a piece of torn newspaper with trembling fingers. Her face was chalk-white as she handed it to him.

His eyes narrowed as he read the ugly printed words. "When did you get this?"

"It came in the mail yesterday." She drew a steadying breath. "I called my grandmother and…and…"

"And what?" Brian prompted.

Robyn swallowed hard. "She dismissed it. Said it must have come from someone who hadn't received an invitation and wanted to spoil the party." Robyn's eyes searched his face. "What do you think?"

She was waiting for his reassurance, but he had none to give her. Every gut instinct told him this was more than the work of a disappointed partygoer.

"Could I keep this?" he asked. "I have a detective friend who might be able to get us a fingerprint."

If Karl Koleski was up to his old pattern of harassment, he might have been careless enough to handle the clipping—and the wreath. Revenge for a celebration of the house he had desperately wanted to be his might be his motive.

"I asked Grandmother if we should call the police," Robyn replied quickly. "She was adamant about not telling anyone. I promised to keep quiet about it. I don't trust anyone to keep it secret—except you," she added as she took the clipping out of his hands and put it in the drawer. "If I send this to the police, there'll be all kinds of questions."

"What about the threatening funeral wreath? Are you supposed to ignore that, too?"

She paled. "It must be the work of the same person. And this time they've actually been to the house. Why would anyone go to such lengths?"

"If we knew that, we'd know who's responsible. Motive—that's always the key." He stopped himself from expanding on the subject. Instead, he said, "I think increased security is a good idea. If someone's going to try to stop the party, it will probably be the night before."

"I don't understand any of this." She bit her lower lip. "I don't know whom to trust these days."

Her words brought a tightness to his chest. Whether or not he was successful in his investigation, his motive for being at Stoneview was going to come out sooner or later. His deception would shatter any feelings she had for him, and what was worse, his deceit would likely reinforce the protective shell she had put around herself. Becoming involved with her would be a selfish act, and one likely to haunt him forever.

"What are you thinking?" she demanded as she moved closer to him. "I want to—" She broke off as a teasing voice from the library doorway startled them both.

"Well, well, look who came home. I knew you two would make a day—or was it a night?—of it," Melva added with a knowing grin as she came in. She eyed Robyn's off-the-shoulder blouse and short skirt. "Funny, I could have sworn you were wearing a slack suit when you left this morning."

"It's a long story," Robyn answered evenly.

"Really?" the woman pressed in an inviting tone.

Ignoring her obvious curiosity, Robyn asked, "How did things go here?"

"All right, I guess, but we had one surprise. Sybil showed up. Apparently Darrel had to stay an extra day in New York, so she decided to come back ahead of him because of Becky. I don't know why. Heaven knows, I've looked after the child plenty of times."

Brian could tell Robyn wasn't happy about having another guest in the house two days early. He couldn't help but wonder if Becky was the real reason Sybil had come back earlier, or if the conversation he'd overheard with Nick had something to do with it.

"She took the bedroom next to the master suite," Melva continued. "And I moved Becky in with me. That way we'll still have the same number of bedrooms free."

Robyn said tiredly, "Well, I think I'll head for a shower and bed."

Brian nodded in agreement. "I'll take care of everything."

The draining emotions of the day had taken their toll on her.

When they were in the hall, out of Melva's sight, he kissed her lightly. "Get some sleep. We'll straighten all this out tomorrow."

She gave him a wry smile. "You don't lie very well."

As he watched her walked away, he resisted the temptation to tell her how wrong she was.

Melva was leaning back against the desk, watching the door, when he came back in the library. Her teasing, gossipy manner was gone.

"Out with it," she ordered in a possessive, motherly

tone. "Robyn looked absolutely green around the gills. What did you do to her? What happened?"

Brian debated. Should he level with Melva about the wreath? Maybe she'd be shocked enough to reveal some valuable insight or information. It was worth a gamble.

"Would you really like to know?" Brian parried. "Come with me and I'll show you."

They went out the front door and followed the path around the house to the back. As they turned the corner, he started to raise his hand to point out the wreath.

Instead he froze, staring at the spot where it had hung.

"I'll be—!" He swore briefly. "It's gone."

Melva looked at him as if he'd lost his mind. "What's gone?"

"A funeral wreath of dead flowers," Brian answered, frowning. "It was hanging on the door when we arrived home." *Had the same person who hung it there taken it away?*

"Why would anyone want to do something like that?" She was openly skeptical. "Are you sure you two weren't seeing things?"

"Robyn was terrified enough to let out a scream hard enough to curdle your blood," he insisted.

"So that's what I heard. I thought it was a cry of one of those annoying loons." Her wide eyes swept the encircling shrubs and trees. "Do you think the nut is still around?"

"I doubt it." *Unless it was someone in the house— such as you.*

Melva's appearance in the library met the time

sequence of their arrival and the obvious removal of the wreath. She could have done it, Brian speculated. Or Karl Koleski could have parked somewhere along the access road, hung the wreath, witnessed Robyn's reaction and then sped off with it. It was too dark to search the grounds now for evidence of the perpetrator.

Melva had recovered from her initial reaction, and in typical fashion began to make light of the whole incident.

"It was probably just some kids having fun. We used to hang out at the cemetery when I was in grade school." She gave an amused chuckle. "We thought we were brave. Something like this would have been right up our alley."

I hope you're right.

Brian escorted Melva inside the house, and told her to make sure the door was locked. Then he headed for the cottage. The lights in the kitchen were on. Because the place had been dark when they arrived, he'd assumed Nick was gone. Had he just returned or had he been there all the time?

"Well, look who's here," Nick said in greeting. Sitting at the table, he had his feet up on another chair and was drinking a beer. "Spent the day with the lady of the house, did you?" His suggestive smile was easy to read. "All work and no play?"

"Mostly," Brian answered in a noncommittal tone. "What have you been up to?"

"Helped a couple of guys finish up the boathouse. Looks good. I think her majesty will be satisfied. A delivery truck brought an order of fireworks that should light up the whole damn lake. I'll tell you one thing, I'm not going out in some boat to light the blasted things."

"Is that what they have planned?" Brian reached in the fridge and took out a beer.

Brian let Nick guide the conversation for a while. Apparently, he'd just returned from having a bite to eat with the two men he'd hired as bodyguards. "It's a damn waste of money if you ask me," he repeated in a surly tone.

"Maybe not. Didn't the Sheldons have a bit of trouble with somebody named Koleski after they moved in here?"

"Where'd you hear about that?" Nick asked, scowling.

"I think Melva mentioned it," Brian lied. "Something about a distant member of the Koleski family raising hell because the Sheldons outbid him when the Parkers put Stoneview up for sale."

"Yeah, Karl Koleski. Crazy, he was. We had to call the law on him." Nick stared at his half-empty bottle of beer. "He vowed to get even. And maybe he did."

"What do you mean?" Brian asked.

"He could have taken the baby, and been the bastard who killed Heather. They never found any of the ransom money on him—but that doesn't mean anything."

"Have you seen anybody hanging around the house? Someone who might be Koleski?"

Nick leaned forward in his chair. "What in the hell are you talking about?"

Brian knew he might as well tell Nick about the funeral wreath before he heard it from Melva. There was no chance of the woman keeping quiet. Another reason for Robyn to be furious with him.

Brian leveled with Nick. "Somebody is harassing Robyn to call off the birthday celebration. An ugly wreath of dead flowers was hanging on the back door when we got back. She received a warning note earlier in the mail, threatening to turn the party into a funeral."

Nick's mouth sagged, and his bafflement seemed totally genuine. Letting out some choice swear words, he set his beer bottle down with a bang. "What kind of slime would do something like that?"

"Nick, did you see anybody on foot, or a car on the access road near here within the last hour?" Brian prodded. "Someone removed the wreath during the few minutes I was in the house."

Nick was on his feet in a second. "Why are we sitting here yapping when we ought to be out looking for the bastard?"

Brian motioned him back down in his chair. "Where are you going to look? The thickly wooded areas of the estate? On the lake? Or maybe drive thirty miles around to Chataqua? If it is Koleski, he's not going to be hanging around. And if it isn't him, who in the blazes are we looking for?"

"Damn!" Nick scowled. "I feel like I ought to do something. This is all going to be my fault, you can bet on it. One more day before the old lady gets here, and then all hell's going to break loose."

ROBYN SAT ON THE EDGE of her bed, hugging herself and staring at the floor. Her thoughts were so tangled, she couldn't follow any of them to a logical conclusion.

Never had she felt so completely off balance. From the heights of unbelievable passion, she'd been plunged into a devil's nightmare. Despite the spine-chilling threats, her grandmother would never cancel the celebration. Robyn shivered. The whole thing could be a monstrous disaster.

When someone knocked on her closed door, she answered quickly, "Who is it?"

"Sybil."

Robyn's hopes that it might be Brian crashed.

"Just a minute."

"I didn't wake you, did I?" Sybil asked as Robyn unlocked the door. "I saw your light. Melva just told me about the horrible wreath." In a nervous gesture, she drew the sash of her silk robe tighter around her.

"Brian told her?" Robyn knew the answer before Sybil nodded.

"He was going to show it to Melva, but it was gone." She sat down on the bed beside Robyn. "I hated your grandmother's idea of this reunion from the very beginning. Bringing all these people together can only mean trouble. What if some horrible person is still around, waiting to cause more heartache? Do you think I should take Becky and leave?"

"No, of course not," Robyn said, with as much conviction as her own uncertainly would allow. "My grandmother believes someone who wasn't invited is making trouble and trying to get the celebration canceled."

"And what do you think?"

Robyn sidestepped the question. In truth, she didn't know what to think. "Nick has arranged for additional security to handle any troublemakers," she assured

Sybil. "You can talk to him tomorrow about someone keeping a special eye on Becky."

"It's never going to end, is it? The past is always going to cast an ugly shadow. All the unanswered questions keep haunting me. I should have paid more attention," she said, staring at the floor. "Heather was so good with the baby, I closed my eyes to some other things about her."

"What kind of things?"

"Little things. Like her being very adamant about having the same day off every week—as if she had an appointment. I never knew who she might be meeting, and I really didn't care. As long as she did her job, I was satisfied. Then, after she was murdered, I wondered if someone had been using her to set up the kidnapping. You know, getting information about the house and Darrel and me." Sybil turned haunted eyes toward Robyn. "She might have realized she'd been used—and was killed before she could tell anyone."

"It could have happened that way," Robyn agreed. "I guess we'll never know."

"Not unless…" Sybil's voice trailed off.

"Don't go there," Robyn said firmly. "And don't think about leaving, Sybil. We'll do whatever you want to make you feel secure about staying. Okay?"

She sighed. "I'll call Darrel in the morning and see if he agrees."

After she'd gone, Robyn wearily settled herself in bed once again. She felt a strange loneliness. The passionate moments she'd spent in Brian's arms seemed to come back only to taunt her. Even as she'd responded to his ardent kisses and caresses, he'd set her away from him.

"Not now, my beauty. We still have seas to sail."

What was he really saying? You had to give him credit for the poetic way of telling her he was steering clear of any romantic commitment.

THE NEXT MORNING, Brian left the cottage and headed for the garage. A hazy mist hung over the lake, and scattered wisps of fog draped the trees and low-lying shrubs. When he'd parked Robyn's car the night before, he'd noticed another car at the far end, next to Melva's, and realized later it must have been Sybil's.

The timing of the wreath's appearance and disappearance could have corresponded with Sybil's presence at the house, he reasoned. If the woman arrived in her car after dark, she would have had an opportunity to hang the wreath, and then remove it while they had been in the library. If Becky's mother wanted the celebration called off for some reason, the threats in both the clipping and the wreath could have been her work.

The car was unlocked, and Brian carefully went over every inch of the front and back seats, and the carpeted floor. If Sybil has transported the wreath inside the car, it was likely that some of the leaves and flowers could have dropped off, he reasoned. When his search revealed nothing incriminating, he tried to open the trunk. Locked. Somehow he'd have to get her car keys and check it later.

He turned his attention to Melva's car. He was certain

the lady had a lot more smarts than she let on. He'd bet that she was the one who called the shots at the Sheldon household. Her behavior regarding the wreath could have been a clever act.

Melva had left her keys in the car, and it was a lot more cluttered than Sybil's. Obviously, Becky was responsible for some of it. A collection of pretend makeup was scattered all over the back seat, and gum and candy wrappers littered the floor, but no flower petals or leaves. Opening the trunk didn't turn up any evidence that a funeral wreath had been put there.

After Brian left the garage, he began a systematic survey of the grounds closest to the house. He searched for footprints, broken shrubbery and stray flowers or leaves that might have dropped off the wreath while it was being hidden or carried.

He realized that he was at a disadvantage because of paths branching through the grounds that only someone familiar with the estate would know about.

He walked a short distance in both directions along the access road that bordered the estate. He found several wide areas where a car could have been parked, but if someone carrying a wreath had been there, night winds could have whipped away any telltale remnants.

Disappointed, Brian returned to Stoneview, not having found anything to indicate whether the harassment was coming from inside or outside of the estate. He was startled to find Becky in the cottage kitchen with Nick. They were sitting at the table and she was showing him some drawings in a notebook.

"You're up bright and early, young lady," Brian teased.

"My mom's still sleeping. I can be really, really quiet," she told him in a conspirator's tone. "Nobody even knows when I'm out of bed."

"Sneaky, huh?" Brian grinned at her.

Nick got to his feet. "Well, I've got work to do. Brian can play your little games, Becky." He paused at the door. "You better be careful, Brian—she wants your fingerprints. If you're a fugitive from the cops, beware."

"Sit down," Becky ordered, pointing at Nick's vacant chair. She had a pencil stuck behind one ear, her hair was uncombed, and he'd bet she'd put on the rumpled clothes from the day before. "Where's your badge?" she demanded.

"I forgot it," Brian lied, hoping he looked repentant.

"Excuses, excuses," she said in a prim voice, and then giggled. "That's what everybody always tells me."

Brian eyed the objects on the table. "What's all of this? I thought you'd be busy with the attic toys."

"I put them all back, except for the bird music box." She lowered her voice. "I dropped it and the birds don't sing anymore." Then she shrugged. "I've got to do fingerprinting anyway. I'm supposed to do hand prints, too, but the stupid kit doesn't have any ink pads big enough. I've been tracing them with a pen, see?"

She showed him a loose-leaf notebook with several hand outlines and some smeared fingerprints. As he glanced through them, he saw that her mom, dad and grandmother had played along with her, as well as some of her friends. He smiled when he saw some hand drawings looked more creative than accurate, with thumbs a bit big, and little fingers too short.

"Now we do yours," she said, with all the authority of an official. "The fingerprints first." With her little hand she rolled his thumb across the ink pad. Then she took his index finger and did the same. "I only do two. Do you think that's enough?"

He nodded solemnly.

"Now the hand. Don't move it!" she ordered as she stood up, leaned over the table and very carefully outlined his large hand on the paper with a pencil. "Now, you put your name at the top, and then it goes into a file—that's my notebook."

"Good enough. Now we do yours."

"Mine?" She looked surprised, but her eyes lit up.

"Sure. Everybody's fingerprints are important."

"Okay." She stuck out her hand. "Do it right," she ordered. She stayed very still as he did the fingerprinting and then traced her hand on another page.

When he was finished, he studied them.

"What's the matter? You're frowning. Is my hand ugly?"

"No, not at all. It's a very pretty hand," he assured her. "Very unique."

"Unique? That's good?" she asked doubtfully.

"Sure, that means it's special," he assured her as he deliberately flipped back through the pages of her hand drawings.

Earlier, he had thought her tracings had been inaccurate, because two of the outlines showed little fingers shorter than normal. When he found the two drawings again, he studied them.

Becky said something to him, but he didn't hear it.

Darrel?

Melva?

Brian's careful outline of Becky's pinky finger showed the same distinct characteristics as her adopted father and grandmother.

Chapter Ten

Sybil hurried into the small dining room where Robyn and Melva were having breakfast. "Where's Becky?"

"Haven't seen her," her mother-in-law answered, frowning. "I thought you were sleeping in her room."

"She slipped out before I woke up. She must have dressed and left."

"I'm sure she's okay," Robyn stated, even as she mentally crossed her fingers. Who knew what went on in the capricious mind of that little girl?

"She's probably playing happily somewhere in the house," Melva offered. "She'll show up when she gets hungry. Unless she already raided the kitchen." She chuckled. "I wouldn't put it past her to play hide and seek with all of us."

"Why don't I take a stroll around outside?" Robyn offered. "I know some pretty neat hiding places, and an early morning walk will do me good. I didn't sleep too well and I need to clear my head."

"No wonder." Melva nodded sympathetically. "With all that horrid wreath business going on, how can anyone pretend everything is fun and roses?"

Sybil bristled. "Well, I'm going to call Darrel this morning and tell him what's happened. He may want us to stay clear of this whole party scheme of Lynette's and go home." Her tone suggested that if she had her way, that's exactly what they were going to do.

Robyn didn't blame Sybil one bit. How could she when she didn't hold to her grandmother's position that there was nothing to be concerned about?

Robyn repeated her offer to look around the grounds for Becky. As she stepped out the side door, she debated whether to head for the gazebo and boathouse, or check the cottage. The decision was made for her when she saw a movement on the back path and Becky came into view. She was swinging her black detective case and humming.

"Your mother's looking for you," Robyn said when they met.

"Okay," she replied without much interest.

"What are you doing out so early?"

"Pounding a beat," she informed Robyn. "That's what policemen do. They walk and talk to people."

"And whom have you been talking to?" Robyn asked solemnly, playing along.

"Nick and my deputy."

"Brian?"

"We've been taking care of detective business."

"Well, honey, I think you'd better scoot into the house and check with your mother. Otherwise, you may find yourself in detention—and that would be really bad for detective business."

After watching the little girl disappear into the house, Robyn continued on the path toward the cottage. Becky must have left the back door ajar when she'd left. As Robyn peered in, she didn't see Brian in the kitchen, but could hear his voice coming from the hall. He was on the phone, talking earnestly to someone.

Boldly, she walked across the kitchen into the hall. As he swung around, he cupped his hand over the phone. She could see the hesitation in his face. He listened for a moment and then said, "Thanks, Frank, I'll let you know."

After he hung up, she asked calmly, "Who's Frank?"

"The policeman friend I told you about. He's willing to send the clipping to a forensic lab for fingerprints."

Relief poured over her like a warm shower. Not Ginger! When she'd asked him if he had a sweetheart or lover, he'd said no, and she wanted to believe he had been telling the truth.

Taking her arm, he guided her back into the kitchen. "What are you doing out so early this morning?"

"Looking for Becky," she answered.

"She left a few minutes ago."

"I know. I met her on the walk. She said the two of you had been up to detective business."

She smiled, but he didn't. A thoughtful gaze narrowed his eyes and there was a firm set to his mouth.

"What is it?" she prodded. "Is Becky in trouble?"

"I don't know. I'm trying to figure it out."

"Figure what out? Why are you talking in riddles?" She couldn't hide a flash of impatience. She wasn't in the mood to play twenty questions.

"I'm sorry," he said quickly. "I don't want to upset you, but I've discovered something this morning that could shed light on a lot of things if it's true."

"What? I'm getting used to surprises," she said as she braced herself.

"This is a big one. I think we'd better sit down."

His tone was serious enough to stop any further questioning until they were both seated at the kitchen table.

"All right, what is it?" she asked as she braced herself.

"It's Becky's notebook. She's been taking fingerprints and drawing hands."

Clearly and concisely, he described what she had collected. At first, Robyn didn't know where he was going with the description of the hands, until he emphasized the physical likeness of the three hand drawings.

"What kind of odds would it be if Melva, her son, Darrel, and his adopted daughter all had the same little finger characteristic? Unless…?" The question hung in the air as Robyn's mind processed what he was implying.

"Unless…unless they all were related," she stammered.

"Exactly."

"But, no, that couldn't be true."

"Why not?"

"It doesn't make any sense. To deny the relationship, I mean."

"Most things make sense when you know the facts. Jumping to conclusions is what usually leads to trouble," he warned her.

"I'd have to have more than a girlish drawing of hands to convince me," Robyn said firmly. "As far as I'm concerned, all of this is really none of our business either way."

"Maybe." He shrugged. "I guess what bothers me is whether or not this kind of secret could be fermenting another tragedy."

"What do you mean?"

"Maybe Becky is not far wrong in thinking she's the star of an unsolved drama. Whatever motivated her first kidnapping might still be the reason someone wants to stop this celebration."

"No, I don't believe it!" Even as the words left her lips, Robyn knew that deep inside she couldn't honestly dismiss what he was suggesting.

From the time she'd moved into the house, she'd experienced a lingering apprehension that in some weird way the unsolved crimes were not history. In all honesty, she would welcome some kind of closure, once and for all. The recent harassment seemed to support Brian's speculation that somehow the threat of party guests mingling was triggering the ugly threats.

"It's just speculation at this point," he assured her. "We'd need a lot more information to reach any kind of conclusion."

"What kind of information?"

He smiled, as if he realized she'd breached some kind of hurdle in her thinking. "Verification of our suspicions, for one thing. Melva told me that Sybil was dead set against adopting. If Darrel fathered his own adopted child, did his wife know about it?"

"I don't see how all of that would have anything to do with Becky's being kidnapped and her nanny being murdered."

"Neither do I. That's what's puzzling, isn't it?" He

leaned back in his chair. "Well, I guess we'll never know unless—or until—something else happens."

"We can't just sit around and hope for the best," she declared.

"What do you suggest we do?" he asked.

"I don't know. What do you think?"

He reached over and took her hand. "Well, let me think about it. In the meantime, don't do anything that would alert Sybil or Melva to our suspicions. And I'll try to keep Becky under control."

"Good luck. That little girl is wily enough to dance to her own tune around most adults."

"Your pirate captain will take care of everything," he assured her as they stood up.

"Promise?" Robyn knew she was shamelessly inviting a kiss as she lifted her face to his.

"Promise," he echoed.

His arms slipped around her, and as he lowered his mouth upon hers, he parted her lips with a questing tongue, igniting instant desire within her. Remembered ecstasy spilled through her as his kisses trailed from her mouth to the crevice of her neck. She shamelessly responded, with a hunger that had lain dormant deep within her, just waiting for this moment. She knew her surrender was obvious in every breath and kiss.

Once again, with an audible groan, he set her away from him. He kept his hands on her shoulders and was silent for a long moment.

"What's wrong? Is it me?" Robyn questioned in a hushed voice.

"Yes. You are the most desirable woman I have ever known."

"And that's bad?"

"At the moment," he admitted in a regretful tone.

"There's someone else, isn't there?"

"No, I swear it," he assured her. "It's some*thing* else."

"Your conscience, perhaps?" she challenged.

"In a way, yes," he agreed. "And an obligation. Can we leave it like that for the moment?"

"Just don't lie to me, please. I couldn't take that."

Even though she wanted to pursue the subject, she could tell he wasn't going to come forth with anything more. When he offered to walk her back to the house, she agreed.

Mrs. Dietz called to her from the kitchen doorway as they entered the back hall. "Telephone. Long distance call. Your grandmother."

"I'll take it in the library. I hope to heavens she's not going to be delayed. It would be just like her to arrive with the guests for her own party," she told Brian.

When they reached the library, she geared herself for the worst as she took the call. Her grandmother sounded tired but cheerful. "Hello, dear. So glad I caught you. I never can remember the time change. Anyway, I wanted you to know right away that I'm altering my itinerary."

Again! Robyn's hand tightened on the receiver. A flood of protests instantly surfaced. She drew in a deep breath, ready to assail her grandmother with every one of them.

"I'm coming back early."

"Oh…oh, good," Robyn stammered.

"I'm already en route, and should arrive in Boston late this afternoon. A commuter flight should put me in Chataqua about eight o'clock."

"Eight o'clock?" Robyn echoed in a tone of disbelief.

"Will you make sure Nick is there with the car to meet me?"

"Of course, Grandmother." She wrote down the flight number and arrival time. "Yes...yes...yes. I'll see you tonight. Goodbye!"

She hung up the phone and, laughing, began to pirouette in the middle of the floor.

Brian smiled. "Let me guess. Your grandmother is coming home?"

"Tonight. I can't believe it." Robyn caught her breath. "She'll have two days to take care of all the last minute stuff. I won't have to make any more of the decisions."

"That's great. Now you can relax."

Her exuberance paled. "Do you think I should have told her about the wreath?"

"Tonight will be soon enough, don't you think?"

"Yes." Robyn drew in a quick, settling breath. "Grandmother can decide what to do. Nick and I will meet her plane and I'll tell her everything."

"I could do the driving if you want me to," he offered.

After a slight hesitation, she said, "Okay."

Why not? Her grandmother had to meet him sooner or later. She glanced at her watch. "I'd better double-check everything and see what still needs to be done. I'll have to—"

"Hey, slow down. No reason to panic. You've done

a damn good job. Don't let anyone tell you that you haven't. Stand up for yourself."

She smiled at him gratefully. She couldn't remember having a cheerleader in her corner before. "I'll try. Now I'd better alert Mrs. Dietz and the others. The whole energy level of the house will change once my grandmother comes through the door. You'll see."

When Mrs. Dietz heard the news, she exclaimed, "Well, praise be! It's about time, too."

"Lynette's coming tonight?" both Melva and Sybil echoed, as if they hadn't heard correctly. They were still in the breakfast room waiting for Becky to finish her tardy meal.

"She's due in on an eight o'clock flight from Boston. Brian and I will drive her car to Chataqua and meet her at the airport."

"I'll feel a lot more comfortable with Lynette here," Sybil declared. "I guess Becky and I will stay, and Darrel can join us when he gets back."

"That makes sense," Melva commented.

"I didn't bring my party dress and accessories with me, though," Sybil lamented. "I didn't bother because I thought I'd be going back home before the party." She eyed Robyn. "I don't suppose you'd have time to stop by our place and pick them up?"

"Sure, why not?" Brian spoke up before Robyn could.

"It's really not out of the way," Sybil assured him. "We're on the main route to the airport."

As Sybil instructed Robyn where to find the designer dress in her closet, and bragged about the very exclusive boutique it came from, Melva rolled her eyes.

"It's a funny color," Becky offered. "Kind of ugly brown like—"

"Becky!" Her mother cut her off. "The color is brown caramel and it's very chic with gold jewelry."

"I still think—"

"That's enough, Becky. If you've finished with your breakfast, you can go upstairs, take a shower and put on some clean clothes. I won't have you running around looking like some urchin."

"What's an urchin?"

Everyone laughed but Sybil.

THE SUN WAS IN THE WEST when Brian and Robyn left Stoneview in Lynette's black BMW. As his mind raced ahead to the hidden agenda that had been forming in his mind all day, he couldn't believe how well things had worked out.

Whether or not Darrel was the biological father of his adopted daughter could easily be determined with a paternity test. DNA samples from Becky and Darrel would verify or deny the relationship. All Brian had to do was provide a laboratory with some samples. He had Sybil's house keys in his pocket, a perfect excuse to be in the Sheldons' home, and the opportunity to secretly obtain those samples. He could only speculate how this unexpected relationship might impact his investigation, but one thing he did know—secret relationships often turned up unforeseen aspects to a crime.

As he drove, he glanced at Robyn beside him. All day she had been busy checking and double-checking last minute details, and it annoyed him that she was so worried about her grandmother's approval. Her body language was anything but tranquil.

"I'm glad we decided to leave early enough to have a bite to eat at the airport," he told her. "You need time to relax a little."

"I wish we didn't have to stop at the Sheldons'. The list of things that Sybil wants may take time to collect."

"Don't worry, we'll get to the airport in plenty of time. Sybil said their place was on the way."

"Sort of," Robyn answered tiredly. "It's a few miles off the airport freeway. I'll tell you where to turn."

The Sheldons' luxurious, two-storied brick home stood at the end of a long driveway curling around to the front door. Brian guessed the property to be about five acres, certainly only a fraction of the size of the Stoneview estate. Given a choice between the two, Brian would have chosen the Sheldons' newer home.

He and Robyn let themselves inside the house with Sybil's key, and deactivated the burglar alarm. A programmed night-light was already on in the foyer, and another in the upstairs hall.

Brian noticed that a central fireplace was the focal point of a spacious, open-plan living room, dining room and kitchen. As he looked around he realized his apartment could fit into one corner of the downstairs.

"Nice," he commented, as Robyn headed for a staircase that was mounted against one wall. "I guess you know your way around," he said as he followed her up the stairs.

"Not really," she answered. "I've been here a few times with Grandmother, but mostly on the ground floor. Sybil brought me upstairs once to show me her new bedroom suite."

While Robyn was busy with Sybil's list, Brian intended to find some DNA samples. Things like toothbrushes and hair samples from both Darrel and Becky would do the job. Somehow he'd have to ditch Robyn long enough to get them.

"Don't the Sheldons have any servants?"

"Just day help. After their experience with Heather, they've kept a distance between themselves and their employees. Both of them were really traumatized by her death."

"Is it all right if I have a look around?" he asked casually. "I'm impressed with the ultramodern layout of the house."

"Sure." Robyn took out the list Sybil had given her. "I'll be as quick as I can."

He waited until she had disappeared through a doorway a short distance down the hall, and then he walked briskly in the opposite direction. Luck was with him. The first bedroom he came to was obviously Becky's. It was filled with an array of books, games and knickknacks, and other evidence of the little girl's insatiable curiosity.

Glancing at a bookcase, he saw a diary and a photo album. He could hear Becky's energetic voice as he quickly flipped through the diary, and as he read innocent girlish accounts of school and family happenings. No mention of her kidnapping nor her recent detective obsession. She might have taken her current diary with her to Stoneview. The photo album was nearly empty, with only a few of Becky's school pictures in it. Obviously, her interest didn't lie in photography.

Her small adjoining bathroom was painted pink, with a shower curtain displaying a collage of Disney characters. Brian found what he was hoping for on the vanity and quickly removed a toothbrush from a Mickey Mouse holder, slipping it into a plastic bag. A hairbrush in the top drawer gave him a tangled wad of dark hair.

So far, so good. Now Darrel.

Brian stepped out into the hall just as hurried, heavy steps sounded on the stairs. Before he could move back into Becky's room, a thick-shouldered, scowling, rough-looking man came into view.

When he saw Brian, he tightened his grip on a forked garden tool. "What the hell you doing in here?" he demanded, looking like a pugnacious dog ready to attack.

"Mrs. Sheldon asked us to do an errand for her," Brian said smoothly in a conversational tone. "I'm Brian Keller, accompanying Miss Valcourt."

"How'd you get in?"

"Mrs. Sheldon gave us a key."

The man's eyes narrowed, and his hand tightened on the garden tool just as Robyn came out into the hall. She had a garment bag over one arm and a small valise in the other.

"Oh, I heard voices. Is something the matter?" she asked when she saw the man's expression and body language.

"I think we're being accused of breaking and entering," Brian said quickly.

"Oh, I see." She walked toward the man. "You're a watchman?"

"No, but I keep my eyes on things."

"I see. What exactly is your position here?" Robyn asked in her best lady-of-the-manor voice, which immediately put the burly man on the defensive.

"I'm the gardener. Two years now."

"What's your name?"

"Horace."

"Well, Horace, I'll tell Mrs. Sheldon how well you're looking after things." She smiled, turned to Brian and indicated the garment bag and valise she was holding. "I found what we came after. Everything was right where Sybil said it should be. I guess we can be on our way."

Damn it. Brian silently swore. What was he going to do now? He'd never have another chance like this to get a sample of Darrel's DNA. He shouldn't have spent those few minutes looking through Becky's diaries. His mind raced. How could he stall?

Robyn's presence had not softened the gardener up a bit. He still wore a pugnacious frown of suspicion as all three of them went down the stairs. Brian was certain he still considered them house thieves as they went out the front door.

"Brrr," Robyn said with a grimace as the man turned and headed toward the back of the house. "I don't know why Sybil would want someone like him around."

"He doesn't look very reliable. Maybe I should check the back door. Make sure it's locked. Then I'll set the security system again. I'll just take a minute. Why don't you go ahead and get in the car?"

"Okay. We're pretty close to the airport and have plenty of time."

He waited until she had reached the car before he spun on his heel and darted back up the stairs, two at a time. He didn't have to turn a light on in the master suite because one was positioned in the windowless hall right outside.

He hurried across the carpeted floor of the master bedroom to a spacious ensuite bathroom. The glow of an overhead light revealed a large whirlpool, and a double sink flanked by two long vanity counters with an assortment of bottles and objects sitting on one side. Obviously Sybil's.

The toothbrush holder on Darrel's side was empty. Brian quickly opened all the drawers. The only hairbrush and comb he found was new and in a leather pouch with the price tag still on it. Wastepaper containers were empty.

Brian was about to admit defeat when he spied a pipe rack on a recessed shelf by the bathtub. He chuckled. Apparently Darrel liked to "soak and smoke."

Quickly, Brian chose a pipe with a well-worn stem, hoping there was enough saliva captured there to provide DNA. He put the pipe into a plastic bag and shoved it into his jacket pocket. Then he hurried out the room and down the stairs. As he reached the bottom step he came face-to-face with Robyn, who was standing just inside the door.

"Sorry to keep you waiting," he said a little breathlessly, hoping his smile was sheepish enough. "I had to make a stop at the little boy's room."

Her eyes narrowed just slightly. "Did you check the back door?"

"Yes," he lied, relying on his instincts that Horace was more interested in catching a thief than being one.

They left the house and returned to the main road leading to the airport. "The restaurant at the Vagabond Motel is fairly decent," Robyn reported. "We can call while we have dinner to see if the Boston commuter is on time. We'll be close enough to the terminal to wait until the last minute."

"Sounds good. Maybe you can relax a little?" he asked with a questioning lift of an eyebrow.

"Maybe. There won't be much time for relaxation when Grandmother gets here." She turned in the seat to face him. "What if we disappeared for the next two days, and showed up just as the guests are arriving—or not at all?"

He laughed and shook his head. "You'd never do it."

"With your encouragement, I might."

"If I didn't know your grandmother would be after us with full cavalry, I might be tempted," he lied.

"Coward," she accused lightly.

Her playful speculation about them running away together surprised him. Even though he knew she didn't mean a word of it, he wasn't comfortable with this kind of banter. Soon, she would know he'd been playing the part of a villain instead of the romantic pirate she imagined him to be.

Neither of them had much of an appetite when they stopped for dinner. Even a glass of wine failed to make them very talkative. Brian knew Robyn's thoughts revolved around the arrival of her grandmother, and he wondered what the old lady's reaction to him would be.

THE CHATAQUA EXPRESS Airport was small, the main floor of the terminal divided into two sections. Passengers bought tickets at one end, checked baggage and then passed through security into a small waiting room furnished with six double-row seats facing each other.

A center door opened to the concourse and a metal staircase was wheeled into position when a plane arrived or was ready to depart. The eight o'clock express from Boston was on time, and they were twenty minutes early when they entered the terminal.

When Robyn excused herself to visit the ladies' room, Brian headed for the bank of telephones. Earlier in the day he'd been tempted to see if there was a message from Ginger waiting for him, but decided it would be safer to call from the airport.

Using his telephone card, he dialed his message recorder. Ginger had called, and suppressed excitement came through in her voice. The cryptic message she'd left was enough to make the very roots of his hair tingle.

"I traced Heather Fox to a fertility sperm bank. I'm in the process of finding out whether she was a nurse employee there—or a recipient."

Chapter Eleven

Brian barely had time to hang up the phone and return to his seat before Robyn came out of the restroom. Every cell in his body was charged with new energy. He'd never believed in coincidence, and the possible ramifications of Ginger's discovery galvanized him.

In her recorded message, Ginger promised to report more information as soon as she had it, and already Brian's trained mind had begun to compute the possibilities.

"You look mighty thoughtful," Robyn commented as she took a seat beside him. "You give yourself away, you know. There's a tiny tightening at the edge of your hairline when you're thinking hard." She reached up and smoothed it out with her fingertips. "There, that's better."

"Only another ten minutes' wait, if the plane's on time," he said, glancing at his watch.

"You're not anxious about meeting my grandmother, are you?" she asked, a touch of surprise in her voice.

"Only because I might be inclined to offer a few choice words if she starts harping on you. She ought to be damn appreciative of all you've done," he replied, forcing himself to put aside myriad questions racing through his mind. If Heather was the mother of the kidnapped baby, all kinds of scenarios presented themselves.

"It's more likely what I haven't done that I'll hear about," Robyn said. "But thanks."

"Will she be traveling alone?" Brian asked, bracing himself to handle a situation that could explode if he failed to win Lynette Valcourt's approval.

"No, her maid, Maya Lieu, will be with her."

At eight-ten, the express plane from Boston arrived, stopping a short distance from the terminal. The flight of stairs was quickly put in place and people meeting arriving passengers migrated toward double doors at one end of the waiting room.

Lynette Valcourt and her maid were the first passengers to deplane, and as soon as they entered the terminal, Robyn moved quickly to her grandmother's side. Brian held back as the two women embraced.

Lynette was a head taller than Robyn, and fashionably dressed, in a dark summer suit that set off her snow-white hair. Nothing in her alert eyes, firm mouth and unblemished complexion betrayed her age.

A small woman of Asian descent smiled shyly at Robyn. Her round face was framed by dark hair twisted into a tight coil at her nape.

"Maya. It's good to see you," Robyn said, pressing her hand.

"Good to be home," she responded softly.

"Yes, indeed," Lynette agreed, and then frowned. "Where's Nick?"

"Oh, he didn't come," Robyn quickly told her.

"What?" Lynette raised a plucked eyebrow. The one word was almost a reprimand in itself.

Robyn motioned Brian forward. "Grandmother, I want you to meet Brian Keller. He's a distant relative of Joe Keller, who, unfortunately, is too ill to attend our party. Brian returned our invitation and will be representing the Keller family at the celebration."

"I see." Lynette's tone clearly denied that she did. "And Nick isn't here because…?"

"Brian volunteered to drive tonight. It was our good luck that he happened to be in the area this past week, and has been a great help getting everything ready."

"My pleasure, Mrs. Valcourt," Brian said smoothly. "I'm truly sorry that Joe is too ill to attend this unique celebration."

"It's a disappointment," she agreed politely.

"I'm honored to accept your invitation and represent the Keller family." Brian hoped he was hitting the right combination of formality and servitude. He couldn't tell from her controlled expression as she handed the baggage stubs to Maya.

"We'll meet you two at the car," she told the maid.

Brian thought her manner clearly underlined a suspicion that he might disappear with her luggage if the maid wasn't along to watch him.

Not a good sign. No question about it, his movement around the estate and his interaction with the others would be severely limited with Lynette on the premises.

When he and Maya reached the luggage area, where people were waiting at the carousel for the bags to appear, Brian said, "Will you excuse me a minute? I'll be right back."

He noticed a self-serve post office located across the hall. After buying a padded envelope from a dispenser, he put in Darrel's pipe, Becky's hair and toothbrush, and included a hasty note. He weighed the package, affixed the correct postage and mailed it to Frank Corelli.

When he returned to the carousel, the luggage had just begun to arrive. He packed one cart to overflowing before Maya finally said, "That's the last bag. Mrs. Valcourt shipped the rest."

"Lucky for us," Brian said with a grin.

The maid responded with a shy smile. "She likes to shop."

When they reached the car, Robyn and her grandmother were already sitting in the back seat. Brian worked a miracle with the luggage and was able to fit everything in except for a couple of cosmetic bags.

"We'll put those in front with…me," Maya suggested, as if the arrangement was not a new one.

"Will you have enough foot room?"

"I am little."

Brian opened the door for Maya, settled the cases to one side of her small feet and then went around to the driver's side. During the time he'd been handling the luggage, Lynette had been talking nonstop to Robyn. She continued her travelogue all the way back to Stoneview, impressing upon her granddaughter the elite status of those who had traveled to the Bahamas to attend the wedding.

Brian glimpsed Robyn's frozen smile in the rearview mirror, and wondered when she'd tell Lynette about the funeral wreath and show her the vicious clipping.

When they reached the estate, he turned into the driveway and brought the BMW to a stop outside the garage door. If Robyn had expected to have a few minutes more alone with her grandmother to prepare her for everything, she was in for a disappointment.

Nick appeared at the car almost immediately and opened Lynette's door. "Welcome back," he greeted her, adding gruffly, "We missed ya."

"Thank you, Nick," Lynette replied, and gave him what Brian guessed was a rare smile.

Brian quickly slid out of the driver's seat. As he opened the door on Robyn's side, he offered his hand to help her. His fingers closed protectively around hers as she stepped out of the car, and she looked up at him as if she was going to defy all proprieties and kiss him right then and there.

Her grandmother's voice effectively broke the magnetic connection between them. "Robyn, help Maya with my small cases. The men can bring in the rest."

A flash of defiance crossed Robyn's face, and for a split second he thought she was going to deny the order, but that moment, Nick came around the back of the car.

"Give me the keys, Brian. I'll open the trunk." Nick's sharp gaze settled on the two of them as if he sensed he'd interrupted something. Robyn quickly withdrew her hand and walked away.

THE LIGHTS WERE ON in the living room, and Melva stepped out into the front hall as Lynette, Robyn and Maya came in.

"It's great to have you back, Lynette," Melva gushed. As if she were the hostess of the house, she motioned her into the living room. "Sit yourself down and relax. You must be exhausted. Traveling is really an endurance contest, don't you think?"

Robyn secretly smiled as Lynette waved the question away. "It depends upon one's perspective, I imagine."

Sybil rose from a chair in front of the fireplace. "I'm so glad you're home. Robyn's had her hands full."

Mrs. Dietz had been hovering in a corner of the room. To Robyn's surprise the housekeeper stepped forward and shook her finger at Lynette. "Too much on your granddaughter's shoulders. Time you come home."

"Well, it's nice to know I was missed," Lynette answered dryly. "I'm sure you didn't have any trouble being first in command while I was gone, Olga. I knew everything was in your capable hands."

"Maybe I quit, what then?" Olga took the small cosmetic case Robyn had been carrying, nodded at Maya to follow her, and marched out of the room.

"She's not serious, is she?" Lynette asked as she turned to Robyn. "This definitely would not be a good time to look for another housekeeper."

"Then you'd better let Mrs. Dietz know you're in her debt for all she's done while you've been gone," she answered firmly.

A tea cart had been set up near Lynette's favorite chair, and Melva and Sybil took seats nearby as they listened to her account of the "absolutely divine wedding."

Robyn chose a place beside Becky on a nearby couch. The little girl had been sneaking rum cookies off a platter while she thought everybody's attention was elsewhere. Robyn spied several hidden under the book on her lap when she dropped down on the couch beside her.

"Are they any good?" she whispered quietly.

Becky tried for a look of innocence. "What?"

"The cookies under your book."

An expression of admiration brightened the little girl's brown eyes. "You want to be one of my detectives?"

"I don't think so, honey," Robyn replied, smiling. "But thanks for asking."

"I know who put the funeral wreath on the door."

Robyn's stomach took a dive, and her breath caught in her throat. "You do? Who, Becky?"

Leaning closer, the little girl whispered, "A vampire. They rob graves."

Robyn tried to smile, but it wasn't easy. Had she really expected the little detective to give her some vital information? She felt totally stupid.

Unfortunately, Sybil had been keeping one ear on her daughter's conversation. "Don't make up stories like that, Becky," she chastised. "It was a living, breathing devil who did it."

"Did what?" Lynette demanded, obviously startled that the conversation had suddenly careened in an entirely unexpected direction.

"I'll tell you later, Grandmother," Robyn hedged.

Sybil was having none of it. "No, now, Robyn. I called Darrel, and he agrees that Lynette needs to make a decision whether or not to go ahead with the celebration."

Melva nodded. "I'm sorry, Lynette. You know I've always been right there, ready to help and plan whatever was on your mind, but this is different. I mean, my memory is not that short." She shot a glance at Becky, whose bright eyes were taking in the whole exchange with obvious delight.

"What on earth are you babbling about, Melva? Would someone please explain."

"There was a funeral wreath on the front door. Robyn saw it, but when we went to look for it a few minutes later, it was gone!" Melva explained. "Someone is warning us there's going to be a funeral if we have the party."

"Utter nonsense!" Lynette snapped. "Robyn, I thought I told you to keep quiet about that stupid warning you got in the mail."

"What warning?" Sybil and Melva demanded, almost in unison.

Lynette obviously realized too late they didn't know about the newspaper clipping. Since her grandmother had brought the subject up, she could darn well do the explaining, Robyn decided. "I haven't said a word to anyone about the letter," she lied. *Brian didn't count.*

"Well, simply put, ladies," Lynette said curtly, addressing Melva and Sybil, "someone who wasn't included in the guest list tore a clipping about the event from the newspaper, printed some ugly words on it and mailed it. Obviously, the prank of the funeral wreath is the work of the same disgruntled person. I certainly would not for one minute give any credence to such adolescent behavior."

Robyn had to admire her grandmother's controlling techniques. Lynette's dismissal of the whole thing implied that anyone who disagreed lacked the intelligence to see the problem as it really was. Melva and Sybil recognized the insinuation and kept any skepticism to themselves.

"It's the kidnapper," Becky interjected. "He's come back."

"Don't be ridiculous, child." Lynette scowled at her, but had little apparent affect on Becky's train of thought.

"He doesn't want a lot of people around," the girl explained. "He wants to scare everybody off. That way he can return to the scene of the crime. He probably forgot something. In my detective manual—"

"That's enough, Becky," Sybil said sternly. "Lynette, you'll have to forgive my daughter. Ever since she got a 'Become a Detective' kit, she's been playing an annoying game."

"It's not a game." Becky protested with all the indignity of an eleven-year-old. "I'm on a case."

Lynette managed a dismissing smile, but Robyn could tell she wasn't amused. Her grandmother's sense of humor rarely extended to anything that wasn't in line with her plans.

Melva's forehead puckered in a frown. "What are we going to do about this harassment?"

"Nothing," Lynette answered sharply. "At least

nothing until after this weekend's celebration. I'm not going to have the party overshadowed by wild tales that would have the police and reporters camping on our doorstep. If the harassment continues, I'll file a complaint." She sighed and rose to her feet. "It's been a long day. Robyn, I'd like a few minutes with you in the library before I retire."

Robyn knew that when her grandmother closed the library door behind them, the topic of conversation wasn't going to be about table decorations and party favors.

"Is there something you want to tell me?" Lynette asked in her no-nonsense tone when they were alone.

"About what?"

"This fellow, Brian Keller?"

"I don't know what you mean."

"Don't play dumb with me, Robyn. I know you too well. Something changes in your face every time you look at him. What's going on here?"

"Nothing, for heaven's sake! Can't I like someone without you giving me the third degree?"

"It depends. What do you know about him?"

"I told you. He's a distant relative of Joe Keller."

"That's it?"

"I think he has a consulting business of some sort—"

"You think?"

"I didn't ask for a Dunn and Bradstreet report, if that's what you want to know," Robyn answered testily.

"And he just showed up here, days ahead of the celebration?"

"He was on vacation in the area, stopped to say

hello, and stayed to help out with the preparations. And God knows, we needed his help."

Robyn quickly told her how Brian helped Nick repair damage caused by the winter ice storm.

"What about the boats?"

"Too damaged to repair. They hauled them away."

"But we'll need one for the fireworks on the lake."

Welcome to the never-never land of problems and crises, Grandmother. Aloud, Robyn said, "I talked to Todd Parker about bringing his cruiser. He's willing to be responsible for the display."

Lynette smiled. "He's such a nice man. I'm glad he's still on the scene." Her voice softened. "Robyn, dear, you really haven't treated h:m very well. If only—"

"If only you would let me run my own life, Grandmother."

Her smile faded. "Run it—or ruin it?"

"Either way, it's my life."

"Really? Well, well, Robyn, I sense some startling changes in you. Is, by any chance, Brian Keller responsible for your adoption of this kind of *c'est la vie* philosophy?"

Robyn wanted to lie and pretend she'd come to an independent declaration on her own, but she knew Brian was the stimulus for her looking at life in a different way. To deny the truth would be some kind of betrayal, so she simply nodded.

"In that case, I think it's my responsibility to make some inquiries about this Brian Keller."

"Grandmother!"

"I'll turn it over to some investigators tomorrow," she answered firmly. "If this man is an upstanding, eligible suitor, with the proper background, it will be verified. Robyn, I trust your good sense and upbringing will win out over a momentary infatuation if the facts show your affections have been misplaced."

"Fine, Grandmother. By all means, do all the investigating you want. I don't even know if Brian is interested in pursuing any kind of future relationship, but I trust his honesty. He stands head and shoulders above anybody I've met so far, and I hope you'll take the time to get to know him."

"Indeed, I will," Lynette answered dryly. "Indeed, I will."

WHEN BRIAN AND NICK CAME downstairs after having delivered Lynette's luggage to the master suite, the family parlor was empty and the library doors closed. Brian's hope to have a little more time with Robyn faded.

When they reached the cottage, Nick pulled out a couple of beers from the refrigerator and motioned for Brian to have a seat at the kitchen table. "We need to have a talk, fellow," he said without preamble. "If you got eyes on Robyn Valcourt, you're fixing to stir up a hornet's nest."

"Really?" Brian leaned back in his chair. "What makes you think I have?"

"I saw the way you were looking at each other. You two have been sparkin' right under everybody's nose, haven't you?" He shook his head. "I should have known it. You two running off to Portland the way you did. And her wanting you to drive to the airport." He pointed a callused finger at Brian. "But the party's over. I'm warning you. That old lady will carve you into little pieces. You'll have trouble lifting your head up when she's through. I've seen her go after other fellows. I don't want to see that happen to a nice guy like you."

"Are you by chance a little sweet on Robyn yourself?" Brian asked, baiting him.

Nick set his beer bottle down with a bang. "Hell, no, what makes you ask something like that?"

Brian shrugged. "I don't know. You kinda act protective around her."

"Hell, somebody should. I'd like to tell the old lady where to get off, but I'm only the hired help." He took another swig of beer. "Robyn was a lost little thing when her parents were killed and she came to live here. Lynette has always kept a tight rein on her. I thought Robyn would rebel when she got older, but it didn't happen. I guess it's her choice to dance to her grandmother's tune all the time. Take it from me, the only thing you'll get is pain that hurts like hell."

"You sound like a man who's been hurt himself."

"This isn't about me," Nick growled. "But since you brought it up, yes, I lost someone I loved."

"To another man?"

Nick ignored the question, tipped his beer bottle and drained it. Then he shoved back his chair. "Brian, don't be a damn fool. The wrong woman can become a noose around your neck that rubs your flesh raw!"

He tossed his empty bottle in the trash, left the

kitchen, and Brian could hear his slow, heavy tread on the stairs echoing through the house.

Brian slowly finished his own beer. He had been surprised at Nick's outspoken warning, and the unanswered question that bothered him the most was whether it was Nick's love for Heather or her murder that had put a noose around his neck.

Chapter Twelve

The entire estate was like a beehive as final preparations for the party swung into high gear. Brian scarcely caught a glimpse of Robyn most of the day. Catering trucks were parked at the back door, unloading equipment, food and supplies. Nursery vans arrived with a wealth of floral arrangements and cut flowers.

While a landscaping crew created instant gardens with potted plants and shrubs, Brian helped Nick string colored lights on the grounds. Brian was amused to see the sudden appearance of flowering tropical trees dotting the lawns, as if Lynette had brought them back from the Bahamas for the occasion.

"What do you know about fireworks?" Nick asked when all the lights and lanterns were in place.

"Well, I've shot off a few in my day," Brian answered with a chuckle. "What's to know?"

"We got five boxes of night flares to be fired on the lake at ten o'clock," he explained. "Robyn has persuaded Todd Parker to let us have the use of his fancy cruiser. He's bringing it around this morning with a protective fireproof mat to protect it. As soon as he gets here, we'll need to load the boxes on the boat and set out the fireworks in some kind of arrangement for the show."

"Who's going to light them?" Brian asked.

"Now, who do you think? Me and my good buddy, Brian." Nick slapped him on the back.

"I'll help you load the boat, but count me out on the rest of it." Brian had no intention of wasting his valuable investigative time sitting out on a lake setting off fireworks. He had to make good use of this rare opportunity to mingle with the guests and see what new leads he might pick up.

When Mrs. Dietz came out of the house, she motioned to Nick.

He grumbled, "What now?"

"Nick, you've got to make a quick run into town and get some dry ice. We don't have nearly enough freezer room for all the perishables. Half of the stuff will thaw out in a couple hours. I told Mrs. Valcourt not to trust those fancy catering outfits. We'd need another freezer to hold everything they've brought."

"I can't go now," Nick protested. "I've got a half-dozen men to supervise."

"Give me the keys," Brian ordered as he held out his hand. "I'll get the ice."

Without an argument, he handed them over. "You won't have to go all the way into Chataqua. There's a freezer plant a few miles before you get to the city limits."

"Don't worry, I'll find it."

"The gas in the pickup is kinda low," Nick confessed. "I been intending to get some on my next trip."

"No problem. I'll make a stop at a gas station," Brian assured him.

Driving away from Stoneview, he was delighted to have this unexpected chance to make some telephone calls. Maybe Ginger had more pertinent information for him.

He pulled into the first gas station. "Please fill it up and check the oil," he told the young attendant. With a quick stride he headed for an outside phone booth. He dialed, deciding to try Ginger at her office first, before checking his messages.

"It must be ESP," she told him when she answered. "I've been waiting for you to respond to the message I left on your answering machine. Did you get it?"

"Yes. What's up?"

"Plenty. I've got confirmation that Heather was working at the sperm bank. She filed a tax form from there. What's interesting is she was only there for three months before she dropped out of sight. Just previous to that employment she was a nurse to an older couple who were long-time friends with the lawyer, John Parker."

Brian could see where she was going in her speculation. *The lawyer knew how much Darrel Sheldon wanted his own child. He could have been the one to propose that Heather be secretly paid and impregnated with Darrel Sheldon's sperm.*

"I'm sorry, but I've hit a dead end trying to connect Heather with the Sheldons' closed adoption," Ginger said, as if reading his thoughts. "But she dropped out of sight long enough to have the baby and then arrange for Darrel Sheldon to adopt his own child. She could have been a surrogate mother."

"Maybe I can find something at this end." He told her about Becky's notebook, and the DNA samples he'd sent in for analysis. "We know Darrel wanted a child of his own, and that Heather could have been persuaded to be the surrogate mother."

"But why would he hire her as the nanny?"

"Maybe Heather was guilty of a little blackmail."

"Could be," Ginger agreed. "She could have decided she wanted to be near her own child. What if she threatened to tell the truth about the relationship after the kidnapping?"

"I know where you're going," Brian said, sighing. "Darrel becomes a primary suspect in her murder."

"What about the wife? I wouldn't want the mother of my husband's child in my own house," Ginger said flatly. "Is she a suspect?"

"Everybody connected with Stoneview is a suspect."

"When's the big celebration?"

"Tomorrow, and the place is a madhouse. If you get any information, call me at Stoneview and pretend you're from my office."

"Will do, but there's no way I can confirm sperm donors without a lot of groundwork, and that takes time," she reminded him.

"Do the best you can, Ginger. I'm not sure how much time I have left."

ALL MORNING ROBYN WAS kept at Lynette's side, answering questions and listening to suggestions that were too late to be implemented. Her grandmother checked and double-checked every detail. By noon Mrs. Dietz was openly rebelling, Melva and Sybil kept themselves at a safe distance, and Robyn had retreated into her old familiar protective shell.

"Todd will be bringing his boat over before noon," Lynette informed her. "I've invited him to stay for lunch. I told Mrs. Dietz to fix us something tasty."

As if the poor woman didn't have enough to do, thought Robyn.

Lynette frowned. "I suppose Mr. Keller will join us. I understand Nick has sent him on an errand. I'm a little puzzled. Is he a guest or isn't he? His status seems a bit blurred."

Robyn knew her grandmother was baiting her. Anything she said could and would be held against her. Remaining silent or changing the subject was her best protection.

"Would you like to take a look at the boathouse now?" she asked. "The second floor wasn't damaged and Nick has set up the bar and refreshment tables."

Lynette glanced at her diamond-studded wristwatch. "I guess there's time before lunch."

It took a half hour to make it down the sidewalk to the boathouse. Lynette didn't like what the landscaping crew had done around the gazebo. She instructed them to remove some of the foliage so a glimpse of the lake could be seen from the bench inside.

Pausing in the area where Heather's body had been found, she gave orders to place more geraniums there—as if more plants could remove the stigma of a dead body.

"No doubt there'll be somebody ghoulish enough to point out the spot," she said with obvious distaste. "Whose boat is that tied up at our dock?"

"It's a rental. Brian has been using it to go back and forth to Chataqua."

"Melva tells me he's been driving your car."

"Only because I didn't want to drive to Portland myself," Robyn replied shortly. "He flew into Chataqua and decided to rent a boat instead of a car. What's wrong with that?"

"Nothing, I guess," Lynette replied, but her tone belied her words. "Well, let's take a look at the boat-house. I hope to heaven it's presentable."

As far as Robyn could tell, it was. She waited while her grandmother checked the bar and approved of the casual menu. A stereo entertainment center was complete with a variety of CDs. She breathed a sigh of relief when there were no new "to-dos" on Lynette's list.

They had just left the boathouse when the sound of a motorboat drew their attention to the lake. As the sleek cruiser streaked in their direction, Lynette said, "I'll bet that's Todd now."

While they watched, he deftly docked on the opposite side of the pier from the rented boat. His was the latest model, with a small enclosed cabin and a fishing deck at the stern.

"I didn't expect a welcoming committee," he said, laughing as he joined them, and gallantly kissing Lynette's cheek. "You look wonderful."

The older woman preened slightly even as she gave a dismissive wave of her hand. "You haven't lost your charming ways, I see. Thank you for helping us out with your boat."

"My pleasure." He slipped an arm around Robyn's waist. "How are you doing, honey? Ready for the big day?"

"Of course. Let the show begin." She forced a smile as she moved away from his embrace.

Lynette took over the conversation as they walked back to the house. Todd listened politely and made the right responses, while Robyn mentally groaned. Lunch was going to be a disaster. She prayed Brian wouldn't be back from his errands in time to join them.

Her prayers were answered.

Lunch proceeded without any sign of him, and as soon as she could, Robyn left the table herself. Stress—or a desperate need to escape—had given her a throbbing headache. She retired to her room, took some aspirin and drew the shades. Fortunately, everyone was too busy to pester her. She didn't even go down for dinner.

When someone opened her door a crack and peeked in at bedtime, Robyn was already in her night clothes and ready to retire. She stiffened until she saw who it was.

"Come in, Becky," she invited with relief. If it had been any of the women of the household, she would have feigned sleep.

Becky brought out a small potted gardenia plant from behind her back. "I got something for you."

Robyn smiled at her. "That's very nice, Becky. Thank you."

"Brian and I snitched it from the garden."

"Brian...?"

"It was his idea," the little girl said quickly, as if to ward off any scolding.

"Really?" She couldn't hide her surprise.

"Yeah, he wanted to come with me but said it wouldn't be proper. I don't know why," she said with childish honestly. "Anyway, he told me to give you this." She handed Robyn a folded note. "What does it say?"

Robyn glanced at it and quickly ad libbed, "Hope you're feeling better."

Becky seemed satisfied. "I'll tell him you're fit as a fiddle," she said, giggling. "That's what Grammie always says."

"Yes, you tell him that." Robyn gave her a bear hug. "Now you'd better go, sweetheart. We have a big day tomorrow."

Becky glanced wistfully at the bed, remembering the night she'd spent there. She gave Robyn a questioning look.

Robyn shook her head. "Not tonight, Becky."

After she'd gone, Robyn read the simple note aloud. "'It's been a long day without you.'"

Trying to read between the lines was frustrating. He always seemed to avoid declaring any commitment about the way he felt about her. Why didn't he just come out and say he loved her and missed her? *Maybe he didn't?*

For a long time, Robyn lay awake, trying to come to terms with emotions that made her a stranger to herself.

She'd always been amused by young women in her classes who had dreamy looks in their eyes as they stared out the window instead of at their books. Now she understood what they were feeling. The only person she really wanted to be with was Brian. After tomorrow, he'd be gone and life would get back to normal. No, not normal. Things would never be the same again.

WHEN ROBIN WOKE UP the morning of the party, the first audible sound she made was a groan, almost immediately followed by a sigh of relief. By midnight the whole birthday spectacle would be over! Memories of the affair would be stored away in photo albums and scrapbooks. It might also be the day Brian disappeared from her life.

After she quickly dressed in jeans and a white sleeveless pullover, she laid out her afternoon dress and shoes for the party. The misty blue silk, with delicate embroidery on the rounded neckline and graceful wing sleeves, had been worn at a designer fashion show. She had bought the dress in Florida when she'd visited her grandmother, and if anyone had told her she'd be wearing it for one special man, she would have laughed in that person's face. Now, as she smoothed its softness, she wondered if the clinging cloth would tempt Brian's caressing hands.

Downstairs, a strange quiet hovered in the carefully decorated rooms and halls as she passed by. Almost like the calm before a storm, she thought. Even in the kitchen, with all the caterers' paraphernalia loading counters, tables and shelves, a sense of waiting seemed to prevail.

"Good morning, Mrs. Dietz."

Startled, the housekeeper swung around and dropped one of the cups she'd been putting on a tray. As the harsh sound of splintering china filled the room, Mrs. Dietz put her hands over her face with a cry.

"It's all right," Robyn hastened to assure her. "It's just a cup."

She raised frightened eyes and said hoarsely, "It's a sign. Something bad is coming. Very bad."

"No, it's only a broken cup, Mrs. Dietz," Robyn replied firmly. "We're all nervous, but everything's going to be just fine. Sweep up the broken pieces and nobody will be the wiser. Then forget about it."

Mrs. Dietz wrung her hands. "Your grandmother wants a tray this morning. Maya will be coming down to get it in a few minutes. The breakfast buffet is already set out for the others." She gave Robyn a weak smile. "I made strong coffee."

"Good, we're all going to need it."

A knock on the back door followed Robyn's words. Two chefs had arrived from the catering service. They hurried into the kitchen to work their magic. The party was to begin with luncheon at two o'clock.

When Robyn glanced out a window and saw Nick's hired guards patrolling the grounds, her stomach tightened. She didn't need a broken cup to tell her that all was not well.

AN HOUR BEFORE the luncheon, the first guests began to arrive. Brian looked out his second-story window and saw the Koleski family emerging from three cars. Many had the strong features of their Polish ancestor, Hugo Koleski, who had bought the land and built Stoneview. Brian doubted that Karl would make an appearance. The funeral wreath and threatening note seemed to be more his style. Brian planned to glean as much information about the troublemaker's whereabouts as he could.

He gave a quick glance in the mirror and tightened a silk print tie that harmonized with his black suit and white shirt and cuff links. His dark hair still had the power to startle him. The reflection of the fashionably dressed man made him seem more like a deceitful stranger than anything. Never had any of his undercover investigations rested so uneasily upon his conscience.

When he entered the large parlor filling up with mingling guests, he saw Robyn standing by her grandmother at the far end of the room. Even though it was daylight, all the parlor lamps had been turned on. In the glow of an overhead chandelier, Robyn was a vision of loveliness in a misty blue summer dress, with her upswept hair shining like a crown of burnished gold. Just looking at her, he felt his heart tighten.

A radiant Lynette, wearing a pale lavender lace gown with diamond accessories, was, without a doubt, the reigning queen as she greeted her guests and bestowed gracious smiles upon them.

As if Robyn had been watching for him, her gaze connected with his immediately. She lifted her chin slightly as she smiled and acknowledged his arrival. He nodded and smiled in return, but before he could move toward her through the gathering guests, Todd Parker appeared at her side. He quickly positioned himself between Lynette and Robyn, and as the three of them stood together, the resemblance to a family portrait was unmistakable.

A woman near Brian commented in an audible titter, "I wonder if there's going to be an engagement announcement."

"About time," her escort answered dryly.

Brian decided not to join the line of guests moving forward to be welcomed by the hostess. Lynette's manner would probably be stiff and coolly polite. Robyn might find it embarrassing, and he suspected Todd Parker would make it clear his position was more than just a guest. The better part of valor might be to avoid the receiving line altogether, Brian reasoned. He'd wait until he could approach Robyn without embarrassing her in any way.

He accepted a glass of champagne from a circulating waiter, and as he looked around, his gaze fell on an attractive young woman he'd seen arrive with the Koleski family. She was sitting on a leather couch, looking over the gathering with an obvious expression of appraisal. He wondered if she might be able to give him some information about Karl Koleski, and was considering approaching her when her gaze locked with his. Clearly, she was used to attracting masculine attention, and an inviting smile tugged at her lips.

"I'm Brian Keller," he said, approaching her and offering the kind of smile her short skirt and crossed legs invited.

"Erina Koleski." She held out a hand, flashing long, ruby-red nails. As he sat down beside her, she added, "My great-great-grandfather built this house."

"I know. My great-uncle, Joe Keller, bought it from someone in your family who had inherited it."

"What a small world it is."

"Yes, isn't it?" He smoothly guided the conversation, learning which members of the Koleski family had accepted Lynette's invitation. When Karl Koleski wasn't among them, he casually asked, "Wasn't there a Koleski who tried to buy the property back? Karl, was it?"

"Our bad boy?" Her smile faded. "Karl's been going his own way all of his life. Once he gets something in his head, you can't get it out. If he shows up today, there'll be nothing but trouble."

"Is there a chance that he will?"

Her voice took on a hard edge. "Karl's been back in the States for a month or two, though we haven't seen him. But let's not talk about him." She peered at Brian over her champagne glass. "Let's talk about you. What kind of business are you in?" He translated that to mean, "How much money do you make?"

"I have my fingers in several corporate pies," he lied. Having found out what he wanted to know, Brian used the Sheldons' appearance as an excuse to end their conversation.

Sybil and Melva smiled and greeted guests, and Darrel held Becky's hand as if his assignment was to keep his daughter out of trouble. When the girl saw Brian, she tugged free of her father's grip and scooted through the crowd in his direction.

"Hi, there," Brian exclaimed as she planted herself right in front of him.

"We're on duty, don't you forget." She shook a warning finger at him. "Keep your eyes open."

"Oh, I will," he answered solemnly.

"You know what we're looking for," she said in a hushed tone.

"Remind me."

"A secret room. Watch everybody." Seriously, she stated, "The guilty always return to the scene of the crime."

"Gotcha," he said, just as Darrel reached them.

"What's going on with you two?" Her father's usually pleasant expression was strained. "I hope you aren't encouraging Becky in this little game of hers, Brian. It was a mistake to let Melva bring her here. We've all tried to be patient, but enough is enough."

"I guess she's got a right to be curious," Brian murmured in her defense. Becky was looking at him with a childlike trust that went too deep to be ignored.

"Curiosity can be a dangerous thing," Darrel said flatly.

Especially when you have so much to hide, Brian silently added.

The results of the DNA tests wouldn't be available for a few days, but Brian's strong gut feeling was that they'd prove Becky was his natural child. *And Heather's?*

A few minutes later Darrel and Sybil were engaged in conversation with John Parker, and Brian saw the little girl slip away again. He chuckled as he watched Becky bounce around the room, telling everyone who would listen that she was working to solve her own kidnapping.

Her parents seemed be unaware of her activity as they talked with Parker. The close rapport they seemed to have with the elderly lawyer was obvious. Had he been the primary catalyst in the whole affair?

Chapter Thirteen

A constant stream of arriving guests kept Brian from approaching Robyn. Several times he could have joined the reception line and politely shaken her hand, but he decided the farce was too much for either of them. He remembered how Nick had caught the charged attraction between them, and Brian didn't want to gamble on Lynette and Todd picking up the same vibrations. Even though Robyn was only the width of a room away, he was painfully aware that the distance separating them could not be measured in yards and inches.

When a dinner gong summoned all the guests to the large dining room, Brian wasn't surprised to find his place card at the opposite end of the room from the head table, where Robyn was seated. Lynette had made it perfectly clear that he didn't belong in the same company with her granddaughter, and she had made sure he was seated accordingly.

The four-course meal was exquisitely prepared and beautifully served, but its elegance was lost on Brian.

He was becoming more positive that somewhere in

the tangled deception of Becky's parentage lay the answers to her kidnapping and Heather's murder. If John Parker's role had been more than just legal advisor, the right questions might breach the silence the lawyer had maintained for twelve years.

ROBYN WAS FURIOUS when she saw that Brian's place card had been moved to the far end of the long room. Her grandmother's tactics were unbelievable! Robyn was positive that Lynette's maneuver to put Todd in the receiving line had been maliciously calculated to give everyone the wrong impression.

Guests had smiled knowingly at her and hinted that a wedding announcement was in the air. Lynette had fostered the rumor by patting Todd's arm and referring to him as her "dear boy."

Robyn ignored Todd's efforts at making table conversation, and barely acknowledged his compliments. During the luncheon, she silently fumed when she saw an attractive, dark-haired young woman sitting by Brian, smiling and laughing. Robyn was sure it was the same one she'd seen him talking with while drinking champagne. She vowed to make sure the rest of the day didn't continue the way it had started out.

At the end of the meal, Lynette made a polite little speech, thanking everyone for coming. John Parker gallantly responded on behalf of the guests, and several local experts offered interesting facts about the historical significance of the estate.

The Koleski family was recognized as descendants of the man who had first owned the estate and built the house. Brian was invited to stand up as representative of the second owner, Joe Keller, and Robyn thought he looked a little embarrassed by the recognition.

But John and Todd Parker weren't. Robyn thought Todd's father was ready to launch into a lengthy account of the years he and his wife had spent at Stoneview, but Lynette didn't give him a chance. She quickly introduced Darrel, Sybil, Becky and Melva as the fourth family to live in the house, and then thanked them for allowing her and her granddaughter, Robyn, to be the current residents.

"We have a photographer at the front of the house waiting to take pictures," Lynette informed the gathering. "And we want everyone to collect there as soon as we leave the dining room. Once the photographs are taken, we invite you to enjoy the house at your leisure. You'll find that many changes have been made during the years. Please feel free to wander." She smiled and added, "The recreation room, the boathouse party facilities and the gardens are for your pleasure. And tonight, after our evening buffet, there will be fireworks on the lake."

A spontaneous ripple of applause greeted this last announcement, followed by a rustle of movement as people pushed back their chairs and began heading toward the open double doors into the hall.

Robyn had intended to reach Brian before he left, but the surge of guests delayed her. By the time she made her way to his end of the room, he had disappeared.

The photography session was long and tedious because Lynette insisted on group sittings, but also kept everyone in attendance while she singled out special individuals. Brian was conspicuously absent, but Lynette didn't seem to notice—or didn't care. When her grandmother was finally satisfied, Robyn made her escape.

She headed toward Nick, who was busy removing a large wooden sign, "STONEVIEW" that Lynette had insisted be used in the photographs.

"Have you seen Brian? For some reason, he ducked out on the picture taking."

"Well, he's not at the boathouse," Nick told her. "I just came from there. If he's not in the house, try the cottage. If I see him, I'll tell him you're looking for him."

Robyn spent the next few minutes checking out the ground floor rooms, but no Brian. Sybil and Becky were just leaving the game room, where a crowd of people was settling down to play poker and bridge. Robyn could tell mother and daughter were having an argument about something.

"You go to your room, young lady," Sybil ordered. "And don't come out until I tell you."

Becky muttered some words Robyn didn't know a child her age had even heard as she scurried out of Sybil's reach.

"What did she do?"

"Embarrassed me to death, that's what!" The woman handed Robyn a piece of paper with a sales pitch printed in crayon: "Get one now! Only twenty-five cents. Autograph of famous kidnapped baby."

Robyn managed to keep a straight face. "Did she sell any?"

"Yes, that's what's so awful. People have actually encouraged her. Darrel and I have done our best to put all

that horror behind us. Now people are going to be
reminded all over again." Her eyes took on a hard glint.
"I knew having this open house was a mistake from the
beginning."

*Enough to try and stop it? Was Sybil responsible for
the funeral wreath and warning?*

"Have you seen Brian?" Robyn asked quickly.

Sybil nodded. "I think he was hiding out in the rec
room until the picture taking was over. He seems to be
camera shy for some reason."

Robyn thanked her, and as she hurried down the
stairs, she heard music from the jukebox floating up
from below. The room was packed, but she saw Brian
right away.

He was sitting at the bar with a beer mug in his hands.
He was talking to Todd's aunt, Cora, who was perched
on a stool next to his. Plump and round-faced, she showed
little interest in styles of dress and haircuts, and one
would never guess she was the proper John Parker's
sister.

Robyn knew Todd had always regarded his maiden
aunt as a boring busybody. From the sound of the old
lady's laugh, Cora was finding Brian quite entertaining.
Robyn wondered what on earth the two of them would
find to talk about.

Purposefully she made her way around the edges of
the small dance floor crowded with couples. Brian's
welcoming smile when he caught sight of her was a
relief. After the treatment he'd been receiving, she
wouldn't have been surprised if he'd been less than
cordial.

"I heard you were hiding out here," Robyn teased. "And in good company, I see," she added, smiling at Cora.

"Well, it hasn't been easy keeping all the other designing females away," Cora replied, winking at her. "But I guess my duty's done."

"It's been my pleasure talking with you," Brian quickly assured her. "Your stories about Stoneview have been very entertaining."

"Well, I hope I haven't hung any dirty linen out to dry," she said as she picked up a shot glass and quickly drained it. "Where's that nephew of mine?"

"I don't know," Robyn answered. "I haven't seen him since the picture taking." *Thank heavens.*

As Cora walked away, a short plump figure a little unsteady on her feet, Robyn glanced at the three empty jiggers sitting on the bar. Apparently Todd's tales about his aunt's growing weakness for Scotch were true. Robyn wondered what stories she'd been sharing with Brian. In some ways, she was a lot like Melva. Get her talking and you couldn't stop her.

Robyn had never been sure how she rated with Cora as a prospective niece. Not that it mattered, she thought as she slipped her arm through Brian's, and the warmth of his body sent spirals of pleasure through her.

"I think they're playing our song," she said solemnly.

"'The Yellow Rose of Texas'?"

"I love that one, don't you?"

"Absolutely."

They both laughed and shared a moment of intimacy that shut out the rest of the world. Robyn's heartbeat quickened with the wonder of finding someone who could change her whole outlook on life with just a smile and the touch of his hand.

"Wouldn't you rather wait for a slow one?" Brian coaxed.

"Nope," she answered readily.

They had just taken a few steps toward the dance floor when someone called her name. They turned around and saw Maya pushing her way through the crowd.

"Robyn," she said a little breathlessly. "I'm glad I found you."

"What is it, Maya?"

"Your grandmother wants to talk with you—in the library."

"Now?" A flash of rebellion surged through Robyn. She was tired of being at her grandmother's beck and call. "I'll check with her later."

"She said it was very important," Maya insisted.

Brian said softly in her ear, "Maybe you should see what she wants."

Robyn hesitated, as if hearing some note of warning. Even as she searched his face, she sensed a sudden disquiet that defied recognition.

"I don't want to leave you," she heard herself say.

"I'll save every dance for you, I promise. Better see what your grandmother wants."

"All right, but I'll only be a few minutes."

Silently fuming, she mounted the stairs with Maya at her side. What kind of crisis had developed now? And why didn't her grandmother just handle it? Maya had wisely murmured something about being needed in the kitchen, and quickly made her escape. Robyn flung open the library door and shut it with an irritation that was quite obvious. "Whatever the problem is, Grandmother, I'm certain you've already decided how to solve it. You don't need my two cents."

Lynette didn't even look up. She was sitting at the computer, and the printer was clicking away as several pages of text fell into the tray. She scooped them up in her hand and stood before acknowledging Robyn's presence.

"I have some rather unpleasant information to pass on to you, my dear," she said before coming around the desk to face Robyn. "Some very distressing news."

"Really? Have you discovered Todd is already married, by chance?" The question dripped with sarcasm. Robyn was sick and tired of her grandmother's matchmaking.

"Don't be absurd."

"It must be something that isn't in line with your plans for my life, Grandmother."

"Yes, that is exactly correct, my dear," she agreed, to Robyn's surprise. "I have only your best interest at heart, you know that. Your dear parents would be giving you the same firm guidance."

Robyn cut off the rest of her platitudes. "What have you done in my best interest, Grandmother?"

"I don't like your defensive tone, Robyn. I contacted some people who gladly pursued an investigation I requested. Their findings have been quick and informative. And Robyn, dear, you should appreciate the effort I've made to bring a very distasteful situation to light before you succumb to any foolishness."

With sickening certainty, she asked, "It's Brian Keller, isn't it? You want to discredit him."

Lynette gave a deep laugh. "Well, that might be possible except for one thing—there is no Brian Keller. Never has been. I've been informed that Joe Keller died a couple of days ago, and had no living relatives. This man who has been pretending to be related to the family is an imposter, pure and simple."

No, it can't be. Every cell in her body denied what her grandmother was saying. Robyn's thoughts whirled like an off-center gyroscope. "It's some kind of mistake."

"The only mistake is the one you made accepting him at face value." She sighed. "I really would have thought you could have seen through his willingness to ingratiate himself. I mean, really, Robyn. What kind of guest shows up more than a week early? You should have been suspicious from the very first moment."

"He RSVP'd to our invitation," she protested. "His name is on the guest list."

"Obviously, he managed to get hold of the one we sent to Joe Keller. The old prizefighter was put in the hospital because he was mugged, and some of his personal effects were stolen. Somehow his invitation got into this imposter's hands."

"No, I don't believe it."

"Use your head, Robyn," Lynette countered sharply. "Con men are always looking for ways to gain entrance into the lives of the wealthy so they can pull off one scam or another. Just be glad we've been alerted in time."

Robyn's chest tightened as she remembered the way Brian had looked around the Sheldon house when they'd stopped there. Had he pretended to use the bathroom, when he was really setting up a return visit?

Robyn dropped down into a chair. Her legs wouldn't hold her anymore. "If he's not Brian Keller, who is he?"

"My investigators will answer that when we send them his fingerprints. It should be easy enough to get a set from any glass he uses today."

"What are we going to do in the meantime?" Robyn's voice didn't even sound like her own.

"I'm not going to have my party ruined by any unpleasantness," Lynette said firmly. "Now that we're onto him, he won't be able to carry out any nefarious plan. As soon as the last rocket is fired, Nick and his hired strong arms will conduct him to the jail in Chataqua."

"What crime has he committed?" *Other than breaking my heart with his lies and deceit?*

"Don't be naive, Robyn. He's the one who sent the threatening note and hung that vile funeral wreath."

"Why would he bother to do something like that?"

Lynette waved away the question. "The authorities will answer that. In the meantime, Robyn, you must keep your distance from that despicable fraud. He'll just feed you more lies, if you let him."

Chapter Fourteen

Brian waited for Robyn to return, and wandered around the recreation room, striking up casual conversations with several guests. None of them proved to be the valuable source of information that Cora Parker had been, however. He'd been surprised at how willing Todd's aunt had been to talk about her brother's part in Becky's adoption.

"He handled everything," she had told Brian with a note of pride. "John's stuck-up sometimes, but a whale of a good lawyer. Darrel went to him to see about an adoption when Sybil finally agreed to it. They waited almost a year before they signed the papers."

"And it was a closed adoption?" Brian had asked, as if he didn't already know.

"Oh, definitely. John never has said word one about the baby's natural parents. It's better than way, you know," she said sagaciously.

"Didn't the police look into it after the kidnapping?"

"They tried, but John maintained client privilege, and after the baby was returned, they didn't force him to open the records. He's kept them locked up to this day," she said proudly. "He's always said that hell would freeze over before anyone would get a look at them. He's got integrity, John has."

If that's the right word for it, Brian mused. If a baby's life was in danger, confidentiality seemed a little inconsequential. Aloud, he said, "That must have been a terrible time for everybody. First the kidnapping, and then the nanny's murder."

Cora had ordered another Scotch and then, leaning toward him, said in a confidential tone, "Even after all this time, I don't think Sybil has ever forgiven Nick."

"Nick? Forgiven him for what?" Brian had asked in the same conspirator's tone.

"For being lax about security. He was hired to make nightly rounds to make sure everything was locked up tight, but that night he'd gone to Al's Pub, and who knows when he got back to the cottage. Apparently he had an alibi that satisfied the police. Anyway, Sybil has blamed Nick for what happened. That's why he didn't stay in their employment when Stoneview was sold to the Valcourts."

"Is there still bad feeling between them?" Brian had asked, remembering the scene he'd overheard between them in the boathouse.

"You better believe it. Sybil's never going to let him forget Heather's murder. Kinda spiteful, if you ask me, but a woman scorned never forgets."

"You think she and Nick…?"

Cora had shrugged. "Who knows? Between you and me, Becky has really been a challenge for Sybil to raise. She's such an independent little thing."

"So I've noticed," Brian had replied dryly.

"Children often are. We're really hoping that Todd's and Robyn's offspring will do both families credit."

Brian had swallowed against a suddenly dry mouth. "Oh, have things progressed that far?"

She just gave him a knowing wink and took another drink of Scotch. When Robyn appeared, Cora had taken off.

Finally, for the first time that day, Brian and Robyn were together. He'd been enjoying her touch, smile and teasing banter when Maya's interruption had put an end to all that.

Tired of waiting for Robyn now, he went upstairs and headed for the library. The afternoon was already nearly over. As he paused in front of the closed door, he heard a murmur of voices and fought the temptation to knock and walk in. He knew Lynette would not appreciate his interference, and he couldn't afford to antagonize her.

He had just turned away when he heard a woman's laughter floating down the main staircase nearby. Erina! Without hesitation, he spun on his heels and headed down the hall in a different direction. He stopped abruptly when Becky bolted out from an alcove under the stairs and grabbed his sleeve.

"What on earth?" he gasped.

"I found it," she whispered.

"Found what?"

She held up a finger in front of her mouth. "Shh. Come with me."

Brian wanted to tell her he didn't have time to be playing games, but he couldn't crush her spirit. As she slipped her hand in his and pulled him along, he whispered, "Where are we going?"

"My room. I'm grounded."

They went up the back stairs without seeing anyone. Becky took the steps two at a time, and when she reached the door to the second floor corridor, she cautiously opened it and peeked out.

"Coast clear," she whispered.

Brian followed her as she bounded down the hall to her room. He was surprised that the upper hall was empty. With so many people in the house, it was plain luck she was able to sneak around without anyone seeing her.

Once inside her bedroom, Becky leaned against the closed door and let out her breath. "Whee. We made it!"

"Becky, I really don't have time—"

She held up her hand like a policeman halting traffic. "I'm your superior, Deputy. That means I'm your boss."

Brian silently groaned. How did he get into this? "All right, Boss. What's this all about? Make it fast."

She motioned him toward her bed, which was piled with books and toys. Apparently she'd been trying to amuse herself during her punishment. Brian refrained from asking what had brought on this latest disciplinary action.

"Look at this." She held up the music box that she'd taken from the attic. "I was trying to fix it so the birds would sing, and look what happened." She showed him the bottom, which had fallen off.

"That's too bad, Becky, but I'm not much good at fixing music boxes."

"No, silly, that's not what I wanted to show you. Look what I found inside. It dropped out when the bottom fell off."

She handed him a piece of paper. He was puzzled. It appeared to be a faded advertisement for athletic equipment.

As he studied it, Becky ordered impatiently, "On the back. Turn it over."

He could see numbers and a couple of letters scribbled there. The writing was faded and practically illegible. Brian held the paper up to the window to see better.

Becky giggled. "Somebody wrote on the paper and hid it in the music box. The numbers are all jumbled up and funny. It must be an address or something like that."

Not an address, he mentally corrected, and tuned out her childish prattle about the numbers being from a treasure map they ought to go looking for.

He studied the yellowed paper. The sprawling, uneven numbers indicated haste. The writer had been in a rush. The order of the numbers and letters suggested a combination to him. Maybe to a safe? Logically, when people were in a hurry to write something down, they reached for the first paper handy. Why an old flyer advertising exercise equipment? It didn't seem a logical choice unless…unless that was the only writing material handy. His thoughts whirled. Maybe it wasn't a combination to a safe, but to a locker.

A gym locker?

As Brian stared at the paper, he began to put some already known facts into a different framework. That first day at Stoneview, Nick had told him the second floor of the boathouse had been a fitness room when the Valcourts bought the house. Brian had seen exercise equipment and lockers stored in the attic. The ones that had originally been in the boathouse? Did the combination scribbled on the flyer belong to one of those lockers? Why had someone written it down and hidden it in the music box?

Becky was sitting cross-legged in the middle of the bed, and he said to her in a matter-of-fact tone, "We can't go looking for the treasure map now."

She scowled. "Why not?"

"With all these people running around the house, someone might figure out what we're after and get there first. We have to keep this our secret, okay?"

She reached up and snatched the piece of paper out of his hand. "That goes in my evidence file."

He nodded in approval. He'd already memorized it. "You keep guard, Becky, so no one sees it. I'll come and get you when the coast is clear."

He gave her a snappy salute, which she returned with a broad grin. He closed the door firmly behind him as he left the room, and waited to make sure there was no traffic in the hall before he headed for the door to the attic stairs.

From his previous trips, he knew where the light switches were located at the bottom and top of the stairway, and he raced upward without hesitation.

The late afternoon sun sent only dappled light through the small attic windows. Shadows of boxes, trunks, furniture moved like dark specters in the growing dimness.

Brian had only a pencil-size flashlight with him, but it helped him navigate to where the exercise equipment had been stored and a half-dozen gym lockers lined up against the wall. He'd noticed them on his earlier reconnaissance of the attic, mainly because Nick had expressed his displeasure about Lynette doing away with the boathouse's exercise room when the Sheldons had left.

Reaching the row of lockers, Brian started at one end and began checking each one. All of them had combination locks, and the first two were unlocked and empty.

The third was locked. Brian tried several times to work the combination he'd memorized, but the lock on the metal door wouldn't open.

The fourth locker door was partially open, its padlock missing, and Brian could see it was filled with some discarded athletic paraphernalia. He turned his attention to the second one from the end, which was securely locked.

His hand was a little unsteady as he once again worked the combination that had been scribbled on the hidden paper. This time the lock gave a click and swung open.

He swallowed hard as he quickly removed the dangling padlock and jerked open the door. At first he thought it was empty until his gaze fell to the bottom of the locker. A multicolored brocade satchel—like a woman's sewing bag—was crammed into the small space.

Brian knelt down, studied it without removing it from the locker, and then carefully opened the latch that closed it.

He leaned back on his heels. Money. Bundles of it.
The ransom money?

It had been paid in bundles of thousand dollar bills,
like those in the satchel. How had it ended up here
instead of in the clutches of the kidnapper?

Becky had taken the music box from a collection of
nursery toys. Had it belonged to Heather?

*Was she the one who had hid the ransom money in
the locker?*

If the answer was yes, how did all of this fit into the
kidnapping and her murder?

Slowly, Brian got to his feet, closed the metal door and
locked it again. The authorities would have to be called
in. As much as he hated the idea of bringing Lynette into
the situation, he really didn't have any choice.

The discovery of the ransom was going to open up
the past again, with all its ugliness. He knew in his
heart one of the casualties was going to be any hope of
a future relationship with Robyn.

With leaden steps, he left the attic and went in search
of Lynette. Someone said they'd seen her walking
toward the lake with John Parker. Brian left the house
and headed in that direction.

ROBYN LINGERED in the library long after her grandmother had returned to her guests. She went over the
investigative reports Lynette had received, with desperate hope that she could find a reason to believe they
were wrong. In the end, she had to surrender to the
truth. The man was a fraud. Whatever his hidden intent
might be, he'd played her beautifully.

As she left the library, she knew she couldn't bear to look "Brian Keller" in the face. She was starting up the stairs to her room when someone called her name. She recognized Todd's voice and didn't turn around. When she heard his quick steps coming after her, she steeled herself not to give way to her threadbare emotions and tell him everything. Soon enough, everyone would know what a blind fool she'd been.

"Hey, wait up," he said as she reached the top. "Where have you been hiding all afternoon?"

Before she could respond, Becky darted out of her room, with her mother in fast pursuit. "Stop this nonsense, Becky, right now. You are not going up to the attic."

"Brian was up there. I peeked out and saw him come down. He's going to find the treasure map before me," she wailed.

Grabbing her daughter by the arm, Sybil firmly ushered her down the hall to where Robyn and Todd stood at the head of the stairs.

"Please excuse the commotion," the woman murmured, obviously embarrassed. "Becky is making up stories—"

"I am not." She thrust a piece of paper into Robyn's hands. "Somebody hid this and I found it and Brian is looking for the treasure, and I—"

"That's enough, young lady." Sybil maneuvered her past Robyn. "We're going to talk to your father about this."

Becky shouted back over her shoulder as her mother pulled her down the stairs. "Don't lose it."

Robyn frowned as she studied a faded advertisement. Todd asked with a chuckle, "What is it?"

"Beats me. A lot of fuss about nothing, I guess," she answered as she showed it to him.

"There's something written on the back," he said when he'd turned it over.

"What?" Robyn took the paper back.

"Looks like a combination of some kind. Maybe to a safe? What was it she said about a treasure?"

"Something about Brian being in the attic looking for it," Robyn answered, feeling a cold prickling down her spine. Was the motivation for his deliberate and calculated deception connected somehow with this piece of paper?

"Maybe we should have a look. If this guy is sneaking around in the attic, you can bet he's up to no damn good," Todd declared with obvious satisfaction.

Too much was happening too fast for Robyn to find the words to argue. If Brian had fallen for one of Becky's childish scams, so much the better. She needed some kind of retribution for his making a perfect fool of her.

"All right, let's do it." She quickly turned toward the attic stairway with the paper grasped firmly in her hand. Maybe it would be better to face him now rather than later.

They found the stairway lights on when they opened the attic door, and Robyn knew then Becky had been telling the truth. For a few seconds she hesitated. Maybe this wasn't a good idea. But Todd was with her, she reasoned. She didn't have to face Brian's heartbreaking deception alone.

They quietly mounted the stairs and hesitated at the top, searching for any flicker of light or movement in the darkening recess of the low-ceiling room.

"Where's the light switch?" Todd whispered.

She groped along the wall and touched a switch that turned on three overhead lights spaced to illuminate the entire attic. They didn't see any sign of Brian as they moved forward.

"Where's the safe Becky was talking about?" Todd asked in hushed tones.

"I've never noticed one," Robyn admitted.

"Where'd all those lockers come from?"

"The Sheldons had an exercise room in the boat-house when they lived here."

"Really." He wandered over to them. "Let me see that paper again." He ignored the lockers that stood open, and tried the combination with the locked ones until he came to the second to the end.

"Anything in it?" Robyn asked, peering around him.

Todd's usually placid face flushed red with anger as he drew out the cloth satchel. "That conniving little bitch!"

"Who?"

"Heather!"

Venomous swear words spewed out of his mouth as he jerked open the bag, revealing packets of money stuffed in it. His whole body twitched with uncontrollable rage. "That's where she hid it," he snarled. "She told me she buried it!"

Robyn tried to draw away but he blocked her. Years of rage and frustration turned him into a terrifying stranger beyond rational thought. He poured out the venom that had poisoned him for eleven years. "She was the one who picked up the ransom at the drop while I hid out with the baby. Then she wouldn't give me my half! I planned everything and she double-crossed me. The dirty little cheat. She was going to disappear with her baby and leave me with nothing! Nothing!"

Robyn tried to find her voice but only a croaking noise came out. She made a move to get away but he grabbed her and shoved her back harshly against a metal locker.

"No, you don't!" His hands fastened on her shoulders, ready to slip around her neck.

Chapter Fifteen

Brian hurried out the front door and stood for a moment on the top step, surveying the wide expanse of land-scaped grounds. Several people were strolling across the grassy areas, and others pausing to look more closely at some of the recent plantings. Narrow paths wove in and out of clumps of trees and flower beds.

No sign of Lynette or John. Brian didn't know how long ago they'd been seen in the gardens. Maybe they had already returned to the house? Or they could be walking along the lake.

Twilight was beginning to be reflected in the ever-changing patterns of the water as he hurried down the walk. He slowed his steps as he passed the gazebo. The thought crossed his mind that Lynette might have been particular about the view from inside the arbor because she had some plans for it. He wouldn't put it past the older lady to plan some kind of romantic tryst of her own with the widowed attorney.

An embracing couple was seated on the bench inside, but it wasn't Lynette and John. A familiar sexy laugh told him Erina had found another target for her romantic wiles.

When Brian reached the pier where the two boats were tethered, he looked in both directions along the shoreline. No sign of a strolling couple.

Loud music was coming from the boathouse, and even though Brian doubted that either Lynette or John would be socializing with the younger crowd, he decided he'd better check before returning to the house.

He bounded up the wrought-iron steps two at a time, an urgency to find Lynette growing with every frustrating minute. The upper room was mostly filled with laughing, singing, dancing Koleski relatives. Under different circumstances Brian might have joined them, but an inner urgency was growing as he quickly surveyed the party room, then turned on his heels and left the boathouse.

As he stepped outside, he momentarily froze. He couldn't believe his eyes. Robyn and Todd were walking close together on the pier. He had his arm around her as they stepped into his boat and disappeared into the cabin.

It was too early for the fireworks display. Brian could only think of one reason for them to be slipping away at this hour. *A romantic rendezvous.* Bitter bile rose in his mouth. So it was true. She'd made her choice.

A moment later, Todd appeared and quickly threw off the bow line, then started the engine. Brian stared at the retreating boat as it began to pull away from the pier. His hands were clenched at his sides. His chest was too tight for breathing. As his eyes fastened on one of the rear windows of the cabin, a shock went through him. His heart jumped into his throat.

Robyn! Her anguished face was clearly visible as she pounded on the glass with one hand and raised something into view with the other.

A brocade satchel! Just like the one in the locker!

Todd's cruiser had gathered speed and was moving swiftly out into the lake as Brian raced to the pier. He waved his arm, but he wasn't sure she could still see him. Already Robyn's head was no more than a speck in the cabin window.

There was no time to yell for someone to help. He threw off the bow line of his rented boat and started the engine. By that time the wake of Todd's sleek cruiser was already sending ripples to the shore from far out in the lake. At that speed, Todd would reach the Chataqua public pier several minutes before his own rented boat could make it across, Brian knew. He had no way to alert the authorities in time to meet the cruiser when it docked.

Brian cursed himself for not handling the discovery of the ransom money in a different way. Damn it! He'd been so concerned about making certain Lynette's position wasn't compromised that he'd made a stupendous mistake. Now Robyn's life was in danger, and he'd never be able to forgive himself. His jealousy of Todd had kept him from looking at the man with the same critical eye he'd focused on the others, but now everything began to fall into a pattern. Todd had been twenty-two years old at the time of the kidnapping. The right age to take up with Heather, especially if Todd had somehow gotten access to his father's files and learned the truth about the baby's parentage. Somehow the ransom money must have come into Heather's possession, and she'd hidden it. Maybe she was more wily than Todd had expected. That would explain her delayed death.

Brian squinted to keep Todd's cruiser in view as the enveloping shadows of twilight cast a gray patina over the water. A white wake fanning out from the cruiser provided a physical guide to the course Todd was taking across the lake. When the cruiser changed directions and was no longer headed toward Chataqua, Brian thought his eyes were deceiving him.

Suddenly, the cruiser headed at full speed toward the western end of the lake.

"What the hell?" Brian swore. The shoreline there was too rough for any kind of marina. Huge stones left aeons ago when the area was covered by glaciers still littered the land, as did cliffs and granite shelves of rock. The rough terrain had prevented any development in that area. As far as Brian knew there wasn't anyplace to safely dock a boat.

He had been forced to turn on lights in the enveloping darkness. Without a doubt, Todd knew he was being pursued. There was something arrogant about the way he was maneuvering all over the lake. It was almost as if he was playing with Brian.

If Robyn hadn't been involved, Brian would have been up to any challenge. He would have rammed the cruiser if necessary. Her stricken face had made it clear she knew her life was in danger. He didn't know how Todd had discovered the satchel in the locker, but obviously, he had taken Robyn hostage to insure his escape.

Only a few minutes of twilight remained, and Brian knew that once darkness settled, the western shoreline would only be a vague impression of undulating cliffs. He cursed himself for not checking out the whole lake when he'd arrived. A lot of things could have changed in twelve years. Maybe there *was* a place to dock a boat at the western end now.

The possibility deepened Brian's apprehension. If Todd knew his way through the jagged granite rocks and dense stands of trees, he might get away. There were a hundred places in the rugged countryside where someone could hide.

Especially if he was alone and didn't have a frightened woman with him.

Brian knew with sickening certainty that Todd would sacrifice Robyn for his own safety. All these years he must have been trying to locate the ransom money. Todd must have lived with the fear that somehow, someone would come across it before he did. Having a houseful of former owners come together must have really spooked him, but his scare tactics to prevent the event hadn't worked. Brian didn't doubt for a moment that Todd was a desperate man, determined to hold on to the money at all costs.

The western end of the lake was coming up fast when Brian turned off the boat's lights and made a quick turn that put him parallel to the shore. He was taking a calculated risk that there was only one possible place a dock might have been built, a small cove he remembered from his youth.

ROBYN HAD HER FACE pressed up against the cabin window when the pinpoint of light from Brian's boat went out. The glimpses she'd had of his craft in mad pursuit had lessened her terror.

What had happened? Had he capsized?

This nightmare couldn't be occurring. Todd was going to murder her. He'd been transformed into a monster right before her eyes. When he'd thrown her to the floor of the attic, he'd threatened to kill her right then and there.

"This money is mine," he had snarled. "Mine! Mine!"

At first she hadn't understood. Then, slowly, his tirade began to curl her insides with the truth. "No, Todd, no," she protested. "Not you."

"Why not me? You've made it clear you don't think I'm good enough to clean your shoes." He glared at her. "All these years I've had a piddling company my father forced on me. When I accidentally saw the records of the Sheldon adoption, I knew things could be different. Heather and I had it all planned." His face turned ugly. "Then she double-crossed me. Wouldn't tell me what she'd done with the money."

"And you killed her," Robyn finished in a horrified voice.

"She asked for it!" Todd had jerked Robyn up from the floor. "I'm sick of women playing me for a fool. We're going to walk down to my boat, all sweet and lovey-dovey. Got it? And once we get there, we're going to take a little ride. You're my ticket out of here, sweetheart. I've got a gun, and don't think I won't use it in a minute if I have to."

She believed him. Once she became expendable, he'd kill her. Her only hope of escape was to outwit him before that happened.

With his suit jacket over one arm, hiding the satchel, he had held her tightly at his side with the other. Guests who saw them leave the house and stroll together down the sidewalk just smiled knowingly.

He had locked her in the cabin of his boat and started the engine, and that's when she had looked through the cabin window and seen Brian.

Thank God, he'd spotted her and followed in the rented boat. But where was he now? Had he given up the chase?

Todd's cruiser was still careening dangerously from side to side, throwing her off balance. She panicked. What if Todd turned the boat over? She'd be trapped inside. No chance to save herself.

I've got to get out!

Earlier she had tried the locked cabin door, and knew the small windows offered the only avenue of escape. She reasoned that if she was petite enough to wiggle through one of them and drop down on the small fishing deck below, she could be ready to leap into the water if the boat flipped over or slowed down. Anything would be better than waiting for Todd to kill her.

Hurrying around the cabin, trying to keep her balance, she opened drawers, searching for something solid enough to break glass. She found it! In a compartment under one of the couches was a set of dumbbells.

Apparently Todd had been working on building up his muscles.

After selecting one she could lift, she swung it against one of the windows. Glass splinters went everywhere, inside and out. Blood streaked Robyn's hands and arms as she cleared the window frame of glass as best she could. Then, frantically, she began wriggling through the small opening. The fragile fabric of her dress tore. Her stockings shredded. The straps on her white slippers broke, leaving her barefoot. But she made it!

As she dropped down on the small deck, the boat made a sudden swerve. She grabbed the stern railing to keep from being pitched overboard. Todd suddenly cut the engine and the cruiser began to glide. She could barely make out the rugged shoreline.

He was going to dock the boat!

Without weighing her decision, she scrambled over the railing and dropped into the dark waters of the lake. Against the night sky, she could see piles of giant boulders jutting into the air. She had no idea how far she was from the murky shore. She swam in that direction, every stroke fueled by rising panic, until she reached a narrow band of earth where steep, vaulting boulders sunk deep into the lake bed.

Even in daylight, she would have been challenged to find a way through the jagged natural rock wall that plunged hundreds of feet down into the lake bed.

The only sound was the movement of water as she gingerly walked on slippery sand at the base of the natural stone wall. She was startled when a dark, sleek otter darted around her and disappeared behind a rugged rock formation just ahead. Hurriedly, she followed him through a break in the pile of boulders and discovered a small open passage leading upward.

Breathlessly, she climbed from one boulder to the next until she reached the top of a rocky precipice.

As she stood and looked down, her momentary relief gave way to breath-choking terror.

Below, not a hundred yards away, Todd's cruiser was snuggled against a crude pier built in rocks extending out into the water.

IN THE DARKNESS, Brian left the rented boat bobbing in the water a short distance from the shore as he dived overboard and swam toward the opening of the small cove. His intuition had paid off. Someone had cleared out enough rocks to allow passage of a small boat. He climbed high enough up on the rocks to see that someone had built a pier at the end of the cove, and that Todd's white cruiser was visible in the deep shadows.

He stooped down, took off his shoes, and palmed the revolver he had left in the boat while at Stoneview. As he slipped silently from one pile of rocks to another, his eyes narrowed to catch some slight movement in the cruiser. The cabin light was on, but he couldn't see any sign of Robyn or Todd inside.

Maybe he was too late. Had they already left the boat?

Brian had almost reached the side of the craft and was carefully moving forward when he felt a rush of air on his neck at the same time he felt the harsh jab of a gun against his back.

"Well, now, look who's here. I thought I saw a flicker of movement on those rocks. You're full of surprises, Mr. Keller. I thought that crummy rented boat of yours had capsized in the lake. Maybe a watery grave is the best way to go." Todd gave a short laugh. "Now drop that gun and turn around slowly."

Every cell in Brian's body was on alert. He didn't know how trigger happy Todd might be. For the moment it seemed wise to do as he was told. He dropped the gun and turned around.

"Good. I'd shoot you now and leave you for the buzzards, but I'm curious. Lynette was hinting that she might need some help handling you after the fireworks. Who in the hell are you?"

"I don't think you want to know, Todd."

"Don't play games with me."

"Why not? You're going to kill me anyway." Brian hoped to pique the man's curiosity enough to buy a little time. "You've really stepped into a swamp hole this time, Todd."

"You don't scare me a bit. You just happened to show up at the wrong time and in the wrong place. And Robyn, too."

"Where is she?" Brian demanded in a razor-edged voice. Todd could have already killed her and dumped her body overboard.

"That's an interesting question. For your information, she saved me a lot of trouble and drowned herself. Right now, she's probably providing some fish with a highbrow dinner."

Brian exploded in fury. His fist shot out, connecting

with Todd's jaw with a cracking blow. As the gun went off, pain like a hot poker seared Brian's upper left arm, but Todd crumpled to the ground. Brian's harsh kick in his side failed to stir his inert body.

"You bastard," Brian swore. At the same instant a sense of someone moving toward him instantly brought him to full alert, and he swung around.

Robyn's clothes were soaked and torn. Her wet hair fell in tangled strands around her face, and her arms and legs were bruised and scratched, but as she came to meet him, Brian had never seen anything so beautiful in his whole life.

Chapter Sixteen

Robyn sat huddled in a blanket in a deck chair as Brian headed the cruiser toward the lights of Chataqua. His shirt was bloody where the bullet had grazed his left arm, but they'd been able to drag Todd into the cabin and tie him up before he recovered from Brian's knockout blow. Robyn was in shock—both physically and mentally—and she was having trouble thinking coherently.

"We'll call Chataqua on the radio and have the authorities meet us," Brian assured her as he wrapped her tenderly in the blanket and kissed her forehead. "Hang in there just a little longer."

She'd thought herself incapable of handling any more shock until she heard him contact the Chataqua police and identify himself.

"This is Detective Brian Donovan of the Boston Crime Force calling from a cruiser on the lake. I need backup at the Chataqua pier to take charge of a prisoner and a stolen ransom. We should be there in about fifteen minutes. Also, have an ambulance waiting. I have a female hostage needing medical attention and—"

He was a policeman! He'd been on an assignment. Ev-
erything that had happened had just been part of his job.

Her mind was suddenly as numb as her body. Feeling
totally betrayed on every level, she sank deeper into her
blanket, shutting him out firmly and deliberately. She
couldn't absorb any more surprises.

After docking the boat at Chataqua, he quickly
turned to her and tried to take her in his arms.

"Don't." She pulled away. His touch only ignited
the depths of betrayal she felt. Everything between them
had had a calculated hidden agenda and he'd played her
beautifully to keep his identity a secret. His kisses and
caresses had seemed real. There was never a hint he
wasn't who he pretended to be.

"I know this isn't the time, but please understand—"

"Oh, I do! Perfectly."

"No, you don't. What happened between us was
honest and sincere on my part. Now that the investigation is over—"

"I never want to see you again." Her stony eyes
brimmed with tears. "You've done your duty, Officer.
Now leave me alone!"

She pushed past him and allowed strangers to whisk
her away in the ambulance.

BRIAN MADE HIS report to the arresting officers, and
alerted them to DNA samples he was certain would
prove Darrel Sheldon's paternity and John Parker's role
in the secret adoption. After he had finished at the police

station, he went to the hospital for first aid on his arm, and asked about Robyn.

She'd already been taken to a private room and his attempts to see her were blocked by a square-jawed female nurse.

"Are you next of kin?"

"No, but—"

"Then come back tomorrow. During visiting hours."

Maybe it was just as well, he told himself as he took an elevator back downstairs. She was too emotionally shattered to consider anything he had to say. The way she'd looked at him stung in a way he'd never experienced before.

He'd just come out of the elevator when he came face to face with Lynette and Nick.

"What in the hell is going on?" Nick demanded.

"What did you do to my granddaughter?" Lynette snapped. "I'll have you arrested, Mr. Whoever You Are!"

"I think you need to sit down, Mrs. Valcourt, while I explain exactly what happened today and why I've been working undercover in your home. I'm Detective Brian Donovan with Boston State Police."

"Well, I'll be—!" Nick swore.

Both of them listened with open mouths. When he'd finished, Lynette said in a strained voice, "It was Todd? He did those horrible things—for money?"

Brian had never expected to see the iron lady crumble, but she covered her face with her diamond-ringed hands and sobbed.

Nick simply put his large hand on Brian's shoulder. "I'm glad you caught the bastard."

Nick left them at the hospital, relieved he'd had the chance to explain everything to Robyn's grandmother. After he'd checked into a motel, he called his parents.

His mother cried on the phone and his father was grateful beyond belief that the truth had finally come out.

"Thank you, son," his father said huskily. "A man's reputation is one of his most prized possessions."

When Brian contacted Ginger and Frank, they were equally delighted that the cold case was now closed. "Time to celebrate," Frank laughingly told him.

Celebrate?

Remembering Robyn's scornful eyes and bitterness, Brian had never felt less like celebrating. The price he'd paid might haunt him for the rest of his life.

ROBYN ARRANGED TO leave the hospital early the next morning. Refusing to go back to Stoneview, she phoned Melva and asked the woman to drive her to the Deerpoint house.

"Landsakes, everybody's shook up over what happened." Melva chattered away as they drove toward the coast. "What a shock. I can't believe all of us were so blind. Todd Parker, of all people! I'm so sorry, honey. I think it's a good thing for you to be by yourself for a while. You know, get everything straightened out."

Her optimistic tone fell flat. At the moment all Robyn wanted to do was hide somewhere, away from the police, away from her grandmother, and most of all, away from Detective Brian Donovan.

"Who would have thought we had an undercover

cop right under our noses all this time?" Melva shot Robyn a searching look. "I guess you never realized his real identity."

"No, but he's an expert at deception." *All kinds!*

"Honey, he was just doing his job."

"Yes, disappointing, isn't it? Everything he said and did was just in the line of duty." She leaned her head back, closed her eyes and successfully shut out Melva's chatter.

When they reached Deerpoint and Robyn walked into the house, memories of the passionate afternoon she'd spent there with Brian almost made her turn around and leave. But where to go? Common sense told her time and place weren't going to matter a heck of a lot. Trying to forget him might already be a lost cause.

Melva agreed to stay at Deerpoint and be a buffer against telephone calls, visitors and pressure from Lynette to return to Stoneview. After the first week, things began to settle down. Robyn gave her statement to an FBI agent and refused to see anyone else.

"I told Brian you were still recuperating," Melva said to Robyn after he'd called for the sixth time. "He made me promise to phone as soon as you were ready to see him. Honey, he sounded really, really anxious. I think you ought to give him a break. While the rest of us were running around, fussing over a birthday party, he was trying to catch a murderer. It couldn't have been easy hiding his own feelings."

Robyn didn't bother to answer. Melva didn't have any idea how hopelessly she'd fallen in love or how deeply she felt betrayed. On a detached level, she listened to the woman's monologue about how glad she was that everything had come out in the open about Becky being Darrel's child.

"Sybil will just have to accept the truth," Melva declared. "After all, the whole thing was very scientific. You know what I mean? How can any woman be jealous of a test tube? Darrel should have been up front about the whole thing in the beginning."

Robyn decided it was time to be up front about a lot of things. Her grandmother had called her daily with orders and plans for the two of them.

"As soon as you've had a little rest, we can—"

"Grandmother, I think you should know that I've resigned from my position at the college."

"Oh, my dear," she gasped. "I didn't realize how deeply this whole miserable experience has affected you. You're not thinking straight. I'll come to Deerpoint immediately—"

"No, please don't. Not for a while. I'll let you know when all my decisions are made, Grandmother. Until then I'd like my privacy." Robyn took a deep breath. "I love you and appreciate everything you've done for me, but it's my life and I want to start living it."

After a stunned silence, Lynette said in a controlled voice, "All right, Robyn. I'll respect your wishes." She hung up without another word.

Robyn began taking walks on the beach or perching on one of the high rocks, watching the never-ceasing ebb and flow of the surf upon the land. Slowly the ache within her began to lessen.

She thought she was daydreaming one afternoon when a familiar figure on the beach came walking toward her. He wore sandals, walking shorts and a nautical decorated T-shirt. A shock of blond hair caught the sunlight.

When he reached her he bowed politely. "May I introduce myself, Miss Valcourt? I'm Buddy Donovan and I'd be honored if you would allow me to make your acquaintance." Without waiting for a response, he eased down beside her.

In her imagination she had created a thousand scenarios about what would happen if she saw him again. They were nothing like this moment. Words wouldn't come and she found it hard to breathe as he searched her face with those deep eyes of his.

"May I tell you about my father?" He told her what had motivated him to conduct the investigation. "I wanted to give my father back his honor and respect. I had to put my investigation first." He put his arm around her. "Yes, I deceived you about my real identity, but nothing else. My feelings for you were never in question. Now that I'm back to being Buddy Donovan, I'd like to prove that to you."

She recognized the gift he was offering her. A new beginning! He was asking her to put aside the circumstances that had engulfed them and allow the present to put a different frame around their relationship. A rebirth of joy and happiness swept through her. As he moved to her side, his kisses were everything she'd needed to put the past behind her.

She told him she'd declared her independence from

her grandmother and resigned her teaching position. "I want a change of scenery."

"We have some great colleges in Boston. And there's plenty to do and see," he assured her. "And I even know a place where you could live."

They walked back to the house arm in arm, smiling and looking at each other. When they reached the front door, he opened it, and then swept her up into his arms.

She laughed in surprise. "Why are you carrying me over the threshold?"

He answered with a knowing smile. "Just practicing."

Silhouette®

INTIMATE MOMENTS™

The MEN of MAYES COUNTY

THERE'S NOTHING LIKE A HOMETOWN HERO...

After a tornado destroys his garage, mechanic Darryl Andrew realizes that more than his livelihood needs rebuilding—his marriage to Faith Meyehauser is crumbling, too. Will the buried secrets stirred up by the storm tear apart their family...or let some fresh air into their relationship?

A HUSBAND'S WATCH

BY KAREN TEMPLETON

Silhouette Intimate Moments #1407

AVAILABLE AT YOUR FAVORITE RETAIL OUTLET.

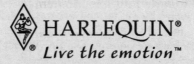

ATHENA FORCE

CHOSEN FOR THEIR TALENTS.
TRAINED TO BE THE BEST.
EXPECTED TO CHANGE THE WORLD.

The women of Athena Academy are back.
Don't miss their compelling new adventures
as they reveal the truth about their founder's
unsolved murder—and provoke the wrath of a
cunning new enemy....

FLASHBACK

by Justine DAVIS

Available April 2006 at your favorite retail outlet.

MORE ATHENA ADVENTURES
COMING SOON:

Look-Alike by Meredith Fletcher, May 2006
Exclusive by Katherine Garbera, June 2006
Pawn by Carla Cassidy, July 2006
Comeback by Doranna Durgin, August 2006